# THE WOLF STRAIN

# THE WOLF STRAIN

## Max Brand®

**GUNSMOKE**

First published in the US by Five Star

This hardback edition 2013
by AudioGO Ltd
by arrangement with
Golden West Literary Agency

ISBN 978 1 471 32110 8

**British Library Cataloguing in Publication Data available.**

Printed and bound in Great Britain by
MPG Books Group Limited

# Contents

"Bared Fangs" under the George Owen Baxter byline appeared in Street & Smith's *Western Story Magazine* (5/10/24) while the serial, "Saddle and Sentiment," by Max Brand was running in six installments — the book edition of this serial was retitled THE TENDERFOOT (Dodd, Mead, 1953). "Bared Fangs" was published two weeks before the serial, "Argentine," by George Owen Baxter began in six installments — retitled THE GENTLE GUNMAN (Dodd, Mead, 1964) for its book edition. There is more than one intimation in this short novel of events from DESTRY RIDES AGAIN (Dodd, Mead, 1930), still six years in the future — and based in large part on the closing Books of Homer's "Odyssey." And there is something more. Frederick Faust's compassion for, and tremendous ability to create, memorable animal characters is very much in evidence in Flinder's encounter with the Gray Shadow. Yet, the final version we have of this magnificent creation is wrenching because in his way the Gray Shadow is forced to confront, as Flinder did during his imprisonment and later at the deserted mountain hotel, the terrifying loneliness of what French philosopher Jean-Paul Sartre would later term *"le néant"* — the ultimate nothingness of existence.

# BARED FANGS

# I

## "COMAS ASSEMBLES TO WELCOME"

When they sent Ben Flinder to prison, he was a smiling boy of eighteen with a straight and supple body and a joyous way about him that was as good as a song. He had his full height, but he had not broadened to the girth of solid maturity. Such was Ben Flinder when they sent him to prison. Such was the Ben Flinder which they had in their eye to see again when he came back to Comas town after ten years in the penitentiary.

Lefty Ginnis confessed that it was he who had killed Dick Lohman. As for Lefty, consumption had left little for the law to do. For him the door from this world was already ajar, but his confession set Ben Flinder free from the penitentiary.

The town of Comas felt that amends must be made. In particular District Attorney Charles Sumner, who had laid the keystone of his fame with the burning indictment of that same Ben Flinder, decided that he must do his best to show his regret. Therefore he had gathered a seven-piece band, including two slide trombones which promised plenty of noise. He had reserved a room in the hotel to which the returning prisoner was to be escorted with music and with cheers. All of Comas turned out for the ceremony and stood about the station impatiently, for the train on which Ben Flinder was coming was already twenty minutes late, and time at a railroad station is multiplied by ten.

Some of the edge having been taken from expectation, it was possible to talk of something other than Ben Flinder and the death of Dick Lohman ten years before and the confession of Lefty Ginnis. So old Thomas Sprague took advantage of the interval to reopen his conversation with Joe Aiken, the insurance agent. All morning he had been arguing his case. Now the diplomacy of Aiken was exhausted.

He said bluntly: "I'm here to do business for my company . . . not charity! What sort of business would it be for me to insure your hotel? Look where she stands up on the side of Comas Mountain, all made of wood, too damned big to be watched, nobody there all winter. . . ."

"Suppose I was to get a guard for it?"

"Would one guard do? I'm afraid not. Look here, Mister Sprague, everybody knows that the Lewis boys have said they're goin' to get you. When they get ready, all they need to do is to step up and touch a match to it. Maybe they've done it this mornin'. Maybe the hotel is burnin' right this minute. We wouldn't know. Nobody'd know. You've stuck your hotel off on the edge of things. There ain't nobody ever goes near it all winter. You make your summer profit, but you got to take the penalty. Didn't the whole town of Comas want you to build down near it, where you'd be some good to it, and where it'd be some good to you?"

"There ain't no scenery here compared to Comas Peak," said Thomas Sprague sadly.

"No scenery?" shrilled Joe Aiken. "No scenery? My heavens!"

He handled real estate as well as insurance as a matter of course. Now, staring at his companion with speechless rage, he gestured toward the great leading points of his arguments which he had advanced ten thousand times before. He indicated the wide and hollow heart of the pass in which Comas stood, green with pasture lands, the mountains walking into the sky on all sides with black pine forests climbing their sides to where the snow began on their bald heads. With hand trailing through the air, he traced

10

the white courses of three streams which raced down from the peaks toward the valley. In conclusion he drew a long breath of that delicious air concerning whose virtues he had expatiated so long. All this he uttered, so to speak, without a word — a silent poem — the while staring at this native of the mountains, this traitor to Comas who had been born and bred in the town.

"It's pretty good," said Sprague humbly. "But away up yonder on the side of Comas Peak. . . ."

He turned his glance to where Comas Mountain lifted its head and its broad shoulders above all the surrounding summits. But Joe Aiken snorted and turned away to gather his wits for a blasting denunciation. Before he could speak, the far-off thunder of the approaching train rolled down from the head of the pass. Presently they could see it coming, streaking along as though frantic with speed to escape from the gloomy heights of the mountains around it. Its whistle blasted the air. It rushed large upon the eye, the lofty engine swaying with labor. Then, with screaming brakes, it drew to a shuddering halt that made the very ground on which the people of Comas stood tremble.

One man climbed down the steps and swung onto the platform. The engine panted, the couplings clashed, and the long train began to groan away from the station, gaining speed so rapidly that the last car whipped past the townsfolk with a whirl of dust around the observation platform. Comas, uncertain, bewildered, stared at this fellow who had come to them in the place of the Ben Flinder they remembered. They saw a huge fellow with Atlantean shoulders who, as he removed his hat to readjust it on his head, gave them a glimpse of hair fluffed with gray at the temples.

Henry Calvin, who was part owner of the big gold mine, had been selected as spokesman. He went up to the tall man and said: "Friend, we been expectin' to see a man named Ben Flinder today. Might be that you brung us some news from him?"

At this the big fellow looked down from his survey of the mountains and the pass and glanced into the smiling face of Calvin. "What might you be wantin' with Ben Flinder?" he asked. "I'm Ben Flinder."

The wind which had been humming down Comas Pass had fallen off to the faintest whisper the moment before, and therefore it was the strong bass voice of Ben Flinder that rolled to the people who were clustered around the station. The district attorney shouted an order; the trombones blasted all ears with a brazen note as the band struck up. Henry Calvin stretched his hand forth to this much-wronged man.

Looking on him with pity and with awe, it was not hard to see in him the slow and cruel passage of the ten years he had served in prison — ten years of brutal labor which hardened his body — ten years of rebellion and hatred which were imprinted clearly in his face. Indeed, the hand of correction had fallen heavily upon him. The governor's order which freed him from the prison delivered him also from the dark cell of the penitentiary. Though the townsfolk could not know such details, they could guess at this and much more. And they saw him brush the proffered hand of Calvin away.

"I ain't come back to Comas to do no hand shaking," he announced in a voice which some could hear even through the clangor of the brass band. Half a dozen of the leading men of the town who were approaching with attorney Charles Sumner at their head to express sympathy and welcome for the wanderer stopped short in confusion, uncertain as to what they should either do or say.

Ben Flinder left them in no long period of doubt. "If that there band was brought out for me," he declared, "shut it up quick. They wasn't no band to see me off from Comas the last time I seen it, and I ain't come back for no turkey dinner trimmed

12

up with music. I ain't had music for ten years, and I don't need none now."

No one gave the appropriate order to the band but, although its tremendous noise walled away the voice of Flinder, yet a spirit in the air seemed to tell them that this was no longer a festive occasion. The drummer fell completely out of rhythm. The cornetist flatted a high C horribly. The two trombones with a final blare of discord brought the music to an abrupt halt. The musicians rubbed their mouths and stared. The crowd gasped and stared also. Ben Flinder strode lightly across the platform and leaped down actively into the street beyond. There was in his expression something of the cruel wisdom which glitters in the eye of a hunting dog when it is loosed in the field and sees game.

The assembled town of Comas turned and looked after him. They noted the excessive width of his shoulders and the feathery ease with which he handled the heavy suitcase in his left hand. Having considered him, they turned back to one another, pale, thoughtful.

"There's gonna be trouble," said Joe Aiken to Sprague. Then remembering the subject of their recent conversation: "You get *Flinder* to be your guard up at the hotel this winter, and I'll see that you get your insurance . . . all you want of it."

"Do you mean it?" asked Sprague. "But," he added, "it don't look like Flinder would be much of a steady workin' man."

"It sure don't look like he would," assented the other. "I've an idea that he'll keep Comas right busy for a few days to come, eh?"

It was that thought which sent men and women and children whispering to their homes.

13

# II

## "PLUMB SAFE!"

The minister was a large, blond, young man with no more fear in his pale blue eyes than there is fear in the heart of a lion. He bore the two sturdy old Saxon names of Edgar Athelstane, and he bore them worthily, being a judicious blending of the two elements of saint and farmer. In his big, gentle heart there was room for all the sorrows of his parish and all its joys also. Having heard of the arrival of the ex-convict, he went that afternoon and found Ben Flinder's door ajar, and Ben Flinder himself stretched in sleep upon his bed.

The good Athelstane was justly surprised. He had expected to find a whiskey bottle, a cloud of tobacco smoke, and the glimmer of new-purchased guns. He had expected to find him savagely upon his guard after so bitter a challenge as Flinder had thrown in the face of Comas. Yet, instead, here was a door carelessly open and the warrior asleep at his post. Was it foolish forgetfulness, or was it rather calm defiance and contempt? One large arm trailed from the bed toward the floor upon which, palm up, lay a callused hand — thick, long fingered, the wrist swollen and bulky with strength. Edgar Athelstane decided that it was haughty scorn which made the big man sleep. A strange chill passing through his blood, he felt for the first time awe of the physical prowess of another man. He was himself big, athletic, well conditioned, but compared to yonder fellow he was a child.

When he called, the sleeper opened his eyes and turned his head. Leisurely he examined the kind, open face of Athelstane and his clerical collar.

"What are you?" he asked.

"A friend," said Athelstane.

14

"You lie," said Ben Flinder. "I got no friends."

The good minister flushed. In his college days he had been an excellent boxer; now the striking muscles lifted into ridges along his powerful arms. He made them relax with a great effort of his will. "I have come to talk with you," he said.

"Step inside, then." Flinder raised himself slowly on one elbow. "Take that chair, will you? Now what do you want with me?"

"Your attention for five minutes, if you please."

"While I'm wakin' up, I don't mind lettin' you talk. Are you raisin' a subscription for something?"

"I have come to talk to you about yourself," said the minister, stung beyond the control of patience. "I have come to warn you that you have begun to act like a fool, and that the reward of such folly, as yours commences to be, is always a broken head at the least!"

He bit his lip as he uttered the last word, convinced that he had ruined his chances of persuading this hard fellow before the conversation had fairly begun. To his surprise Ben Flinder swung to his feet, brushed his tousled hair out of his eyes and, advancing upon the minister with a grin, closed the hand of Athelstane with a gigantic grip.

"Partner," he said, "I took you for one of them fat-headed parsons. I see I made a mistake. Sit down."

Edgar Athelstane drew a great breath of relief. "I'm glad that we can talk as friends," he said.

"We can start that way," said Ben Flinder.

"You know, Flinder, that Comas was ready to receive you with open arms. Comas realized that you had been greatly injured. It wanted to make amends. But you have thrown your hat in its face."

Ben Flinder considered his man gravely, nodding. "Look here," he said, "suppose you was to offer me a drink in trade for this here gun." He took out a big Colt of rather ancient model. The

15

handle was blackened and worn with much handling. "This here gun," he went on, "that I learned on. She shoots straight. She handles easy. She fits my hand like she was made for me. Would I make a trade like that?"

"Of course not."

"These folks here in Comas give me a crooked deal. Here's a gent murdered. They pick me out. I got no family. They don't hurt no feelings but mine if they soak me. They put in twelve men and a judge, and I get life." A faint flush stained his cheeks which were ordinarily the sickly prison pallor. "I was eighteen. I was sweet on a girl. I had a lot of chums. I liked every day mighty fine. I hated to go to bed at night, I was so damned fond of livin'. Well, sir, they swiped three thousand four hundred and twelve of my best days. They give me three thousand four hundred and twelve days of hell instead. And time in a prison runs ten times as slow as it does outside of prison. Besides, there wasn't nothin' to hope for. It was life. I couldn't say that every day took me closer to bein' free. Nope, there was no freedom for me but dying. Those ten years is spent. Comas wants to pay me for 'em with a brass band and a lot of noise. The devil, partner, I ain't a fool. You can't buy ten years of my life for that."

It sounded rather a difficult thing to answer from the viewpoint of Edgar Athelstane, but he said at last: "If Comas has injured you, give Comas a chance to repay you in its own way."

"I've talked enough," rumbled Flinder. "I wanted to make it clear, and I've made it clear enough to suit you. If it ain't plain to you, then you be damned!"

He turned his back upon his visitor and stood with spread legs at ease before the window, his thumbs hooked into his belt. Edgar Athelstane had a most natural and most ungodly desire to twitch the big fellow around with one hand and knock him down with the other. But there was that about the stature and the poise of Flinder that suggested a rock-like ability to with-stand shocks. Besides Athelstane was a man of God. He merely stepped a little closer to the other and said: "Flinder, if you won't listen to a reasonable argument at least listen to a reasonable warning. You have showed your teeth to Comas, and Comas is prepared to deal with you in your own fashion. Mark my word, Flinder . . . if you raise a hand, a dozen guns will blow the life out of your body. Mistakes are often cruel things. The mistake in your case was most damnable, man. But surely, Flinder, you realize that there was no malice toward you. It was an accident. . . ."

Flinder turned about and gave the minister a glimpse of a face convulsed with more evil than honest Edgar Athelstane had ever seen in all his days on the earth.

"Was what the Lewis boys told about me . . . was that just accident? You . . . well, you've said enough. Now get out, or I'll throw you out!"

For half a second Edgar Athelstane again considered driving a hard right fist into the face of this giant mountaineer and cow-puncher. Before the full second elapsed, however, he had turned on his heel and was striding from the room. He left behind him an infuriated monster who roved about his room in a passion of hatred for the entire world. The well-intentioned words of Athelstane had merely conjured into his mind a more vivid mem-ory of his arrest, his trial, the denunciation in the courtroom, the solemn and angry voice of the judge, the black faces of the jurymen, the brutal penitentiary, and the endless and dragging torment of every day.

He buckled on his cartridge belt below that which secured his trousers. He jammed the battered old sombrero upon his head. He knotted a bandanna about his throat. Then he paused to polish his boots. Those boots were his only vanity in dress. They must be tailor made; they must fit the high-springing arch of his instep with the delicate accuracy of a glove; they must taper with exquisite nicety toward the toe; they must be adorned at the heel with spoon-handle spurs, thrusting far out, the steel and the solid silver flashing like an ice crystal. He had given them the last touch before proceeding on his errand of wrath when there came a tap at the door.

"Come in!" bellowed Flinder, and at once there stood before him the undersized, trouble-bowed form of old Thomas Sprague. "You . . . ," thundered the giant, "what the devil do you want?"

Thomas Sprague clutched the doorknob with a frightened hand. "Nothing," he said. "I. . . ."

"Shut the door. Here. Sit down!" commanded Flinder, somewhat ashamed as he noted the white hair of his visitor. "I . . . I thought that you was somebody else. Well, what is it?"

"I allowed that you might not have found a job yet, Flinder," said Sprague very much as though he feared that he might wound the tender feelings of Flinder even by such a question as this.

"I ain't found a job," said Flinder. "I dunno that I'll ever find one ag'in." He held out his callused hands. "I done enough work in the last ten years to do me. Startin' from today, maybe I'll just rest." His smile was a silent snarl of malice.

"How'll you live?" asked Thomas Sprague innocently.

"I dunno," said Flinder carelessly. "Maybe other folks will have enough for themselves and for me too. That's the way I figure to do it."

Comprehension swept over the brain of Sprague, and he stared like a child at the big man. "I have a mighty easy job," he suggested, moving forward to the edge of his chair in readiness to take his leave.

"That's it," said Flinder. "It's the *idea* of a job that I don't like. It's just another kind of prison. D'you see?"

Sprague said nothing, but he sighed and rose. "I was bankin'

18

heavy on you," he muttered. "It was too dangerous for anybody else."

The head of Flinder lifted a little. "What are you drivin' at?" he asked.

"The Sprague Hotel up on the side of Comas. . . ."

"I never heard tell of it."

"I built it after you . . . after you left Comas, Flinder. Sold my ranch. Sunk everything in the hotel. It didn't do much good the first year. After that it came on pretty well. Got most of the mortgages cleared off. But now it's like to be wiped out on me, and I can't get insurance to cover it."

"Too bad," said Flinder through a yawn.

"You see, Flinder, the Lewis boys. . . ."

"What about them?"

"Are they friends of yours?" asked the timid old man.

"The rats!" said Flinder huskily. "What about 'em?"

Bright hope flushed Sprague. "Flinder, they fell foul of me last summer. They was ridin' down to the hotel cuttin' up and botherin' the guests. You know what highfalutin Eastern folks want out here? Lots of mountains, lots of trees, lots of air, and a lot of rough-lookin' gents to look at but not to hear. Well, the Lewis gang could sure be heard. I begged 'em to quit. They laughed at me. I had 'em throwed off the place after five guests left one day on account of them rapscallions. When I done that, they swore that they'd get even . . . that they'd burn the hotel to the ground this winter. Y'understand? I tried to get insurance. Aiken wouldn't listen till he seen you get off the train. 'Get Flinder for a guard,' he said, 'and I'll give you all the insurance you want.' That's why I come around here to you!"

"They's five in that Lewis outfit," mused Flinder.

"I knew numbers didn't mean nothin' to you." He added softly: "Besides, you'd get twenty a week . . . twenty a week, Flinder! Plenty of the best chuck . . . anything you want to order. A fine pair of hosses to ride up there. Nothin' to do but to sit around and get fat . . . just keepin' your eyes open! Besides, you'd have a chance, partner, to think things over and see what you wanted to do next."

"Shut up!" growled out Flinder. "I'm thinkin'."

"If you was to drop one of them Lewis boys . . . the law couldn't touch you, old son. It'd be safe . . . plumb safe!" His face lighted and wrinkled like the face of a fox when it grins at a chicken perched high above its reach.

"Gimme three days for thinkin' it over," said Ben Flinder.

# III

## "MASKED MAN INJURES THREE"

Three men came close to death that night, one in Comas and two in the surrounding district not half a mile from the town. At ten o'clock Jeff Ormond sat in his shack splicing together the broken halves of a cinch. The door was thrust open and in the square stood a tall, masked man covering him with a steady revolver.

"Jeff," said the stranger in a voice so low and husky that it was hardly more than a whisper, "come outside. We got to talk something over . . . and bring your gun with you."

Jeff, with his heart in his mouth and his Colt in his hand, stepped forth into the starlight.

"Shove that gun into the holster," commanded the husky voice and, when Jeff obeyed, the stranger did the same thing.

"Now yank out that gun and try to nail me if you can," said the masked man, "because if you don't, I'll drop you."

Ormond, in fear for his life, pulled the weapon but fired blindly

20

in the air, for though his nocturnal visitor had waited until Jeff made the first move, yet so far greater was his speed that the gun was out and spat fire from his hand before that of Ormond was more than clear of the leather. They picked Jeff up an hour later, still unconscious but not mortally wounded. The bullet had run a furrow deep in the base of the skull along which it had glanced from the forehead.

At about twenty minutes past ten Bill Denny, living on the northern edge of Comas, was stopped by a masked marauder while on his way from the stable to his house. He also was challenged. He also was hurled to the ground by a bullet which, though fairly aimed for the heart no doubt, only tore its way through the hollow of the shoulder.

At five minutes before eleven Harry Kirk, as he dismounted from his horse in front of his home, was challenged in the same fashion. Harry was a fighting flash who could handle a gun as a cat can handle its paw. He had fairly good light, for the stars were clear and the form of his opponent was clearly outlined against the whitewashed wall of the house. Yet Harry Kirk fell as the others had fallen and with a far more serious wound. The bullet drove straight through and through his body. When the morning came, the doctor could say that he was sure to live but that it would be a long time before he regained his feet.

These three startling reports came to the ears of the town of Comas as soon as dawn had aroused them from their beds. They put two and two together and then, after a hastily summoned meeting, nominated Henry Calvin to call upon Ben Flinder. The mine owner screwed up his face but, since this commission was an honorable even if a dangerous one and since he was not without his share of courage, he proceeded straight to the hotel and found Ben Flinder lounging on the verandah, bathing in the winter sunlight which shone dazzlingly upon the prison pallor of his face.

21

"Ben," said the mine owner, combing his long mustache carefully and watching his companion, "we been talkin' about you."

"Who's been talkin'?"

"The whole town."

"Whatever they say about me," Flinder said, "I don't give a damn."

"They was three men shot last night around Comas."

"What's that to me? Do I care if they're all shot?"

"One was the foreman of the jury that sent you up for life . . . Harry Kirk. The two others served on that same jury. You understand?"

"I understand this," said Ben Flinder. "I ain't a man that loves to talk or that loves to hear it."

Henry Calvin continued, unperturbed: "The gent that done the shootin' was a big feller, mighty fast with his gun . . . as fast as you used to be, Flinder. He dropped his three men, and he aimed to kill each time. Only luck kept him from doin' what he wanted to. He left all three for dead."

"The devil!" exclaimed Flinder. "D'you think that, if I'd shot at three men, they'd be all alive, Calvin?"

"It ain't what I think that matters. It's what the town thinks. Y'understand that?"

"What they think ain't nothin' to me. Why should it be?"

"They think that you done the work, Flinder."

"Thinkin' ain't what counts in the law. Where's their proof? I turned in at nine o'clock last night. Joe Dougherty seen me go into my room, and maybe he heard me lock my door."

"We've talked to Joe, but they's other ways out of your room besides the door. They's the window that ain't so very far from the ground that a man couldn't jump . . . if he had a little nerve. They's even a way to climb back!"

"Is there marks of climbin'?"

"A gent that pulled off his boots wouldn't leave no marks

22

with his stocking feet."

"I stay in Comas," said Ben Flinder and yawned. "Suspicion ain't nothin' in the eyes of the law. I've studied it up, and I know. Facts is what count. Where's your facts?"

"They's something besides law here. They's the people of Comas. Sometimes it don't take facts for 'em to make up their minds. Take young Hugh Carey. Nobody *knowed* that he'd been doin' the robbin' around these parts but, after he was tarred and feathered and run out of town, the robbin' stopped. Folks around here have a way of doin' that. They just put two and two together and jump to conclusions."

"If they jump my way, Calvin, they'll find trouble."

The old man raised a gnarled forefinger, deformed by labor in the mines during his younger prime of strength and trembling now with the weakness of age. "Ben Flinder," he said, "when a crowd starts, it don't fear no one man. He may be stronger than any six of 'em. But they work together. They can use a hand that's stronger even than *your* hand, Flinder!" With that he made a swift circular gesture and drew back his arm as though to illustrate the drawing tight of a noose. He rose. "Folks expect you'll find something to do outside of Comas along about noon, Flinder. They don't expect to see you come back here . . . not ever."

Flinder rose in turn. "When I come," he said, "I'll have a callin' card so's you know that I've been here." And he grinned wickedly at the little miner.

With these tidings Calvin returned to those who sent him. Ben Flinder went up to his room, rolled his pack, carried it downstairs, and demanded his bill. The proprietor faced him with a feeble smile.

"No bill for you, Ben," he said cheerfully. "Glad to have had you with us. Wish you could've stayed longer."

"You lie," said Flinder. "You're one of them that has been

23

workin' to put me down. Gimme that bill!"

The proprietor could not speak. His voice had died somewhere in his throat, so he scribbled the bill hastily and received the money in exchange for it. Then Flinder went to Thomas Sprague.

"I'll take that job," he said. "They've run me out of town, and I guess you lent 'em a hand to turn the trick."

"I swear to . . . ," began Sprague.

"Look!" broke in the ex-convict. "I ain't askin' you to lie to me. I ain't askin' you to praise me. You hate me, but you need a watchdog. I hate you and all the rest of 'em. But I need a chance to figure things out and plan my next moves. I'll take care of your shack as well as I can. Fix me up and get me started. I want to slope before noon. After that they got a necklace of rope waitin' for me."

Sprague took him down to the store and bade him order what he wanted. The needs of Flinder were numerous. Plainly he did not wish to fast while he was in that retreat among the mountains. He demanded and received great Virginia hams, great sides of bacon richly streaked with meat, white flour and corn meal, tobacco, and tea in quantity, whole stacks of bottled jellies and tinned jams, crackers, and hardtack, spices, dried fruits, canned meats, potatoes, and what vegetables would serve to keep him in fresh green things for the first week or so at the least.

When this large mass of provisions had been gathered and when old Thomas Sprague had sighed and paid the bill for it, they went down to the corrals where the Sprague horses were kept. During the summer the horses drew the stage to the hotel and through the winding mountain roads in teams of six or were hired out to the guests for their riding. They were selected stock with ample strains of Thoroughbred blood enriching the mustang base which gave them hardihood and goat-like surety of foot through the rough country.

Ben Flinder tried the saddle on half a dozen before he found one to his liking, a monster of a roan mare. Twice she pitched him from the saddle into the air. Twice he reeled up from the dust and went at her again. After twenty minutes he went back to Sprague. As for the mare, she was barely able to walk and no more.

"Her and me, we understand each other," said Ben Flinder as he dismounted. He stood behind her and rested a hand on her rump. "We won't have no more trouble."

"Man! Man!" gasped out Sprague. "She'll kick your head off. Stand away from her . . . !"

"Her? Kick?" Flinder jerked her tail hard to one side. The mare grunted but made no offer with her heels. "Nope. She and me understand each other. I'll have no more trouble." He led her toward the barn with fumbling steps to find her particular saddle and bridle, for she was too big of head and body for the outfit with which he had just mastered her.

"She would have gone along easy enough," said Sprague, following hastily, "if you hadn't roughed her so much with your spurs and your quirt."

"I want her to know the worst of me," said Flinder through his teeth. "Men and dogs, I want 'em to know the worst about me . . . and then make 'em like it!"

With the last exclamation he leaped abruptly back for out of the door of the barn streaked a great, gray body that gave him a glimpse of flashing white teeth and devilish eyes and a bristling mane and swerved along the side of the barn.

"A wolf!" cried Flinder and tried a snapshot from the hip.

The great beast turned with a howl and stood bristling, his eyes green. He skulked forward on his belly toward his enemy then thought better of it and leaped out of sight around the corner of the barn.

Even Flinder seemed shaken by that dreadful apparition. He rubbed his knuckles across his forehead and muttered to Sprague:

25

"Is that a pet nightmare that you keep around your place?"

"I'd've give a hundred dollars if you'd killed it," said Thomas Sprague, still stiff and tall with the recent fear. "It's the Gray Shadow!"

"A loafer that hunts by day?" growled out Flinder, staring toward the corner around which the monster had disappeared.

He received a sketch of the creature's history. For two years it had plagued the people of Comas, descending upon their barnyards to slaughter a dozen fowl for the one it could eat, sometimes pulling down a colt in the spring or slashing the throat of a lone cow which it found wandering, oftener prowling around the outskirts of the village and killing the dogs which ran out at it. There were some who said that the Gray Shadow was a cross between some large breed of dog and a great lobo, since there seemed to be in its nature a mysterious love of the near neighborhood of man. Yet there was enough wolf in it to keep it out of harm's way. Rarely was it seen in the midday as had happened on this occasion, but in the dawn or the dusk the gray wanderer could be seen prowling swiftly through the gloom and disappearing from some errand of mischief.

"He don't bring no luck," concluded Sprague.

"I don't need luck," said Flinder. "I've got on without it for nearly thirty years!"

There were other purchases to be made — of heavy clothing, of stout boots, of snowshoes, of liberal quantities of ammunition for rifle and revolver, of two great-bladed hunting knives of fine gray steel, and a score of minor essentials, or what appeared essentials to the luxurious mind of Flinder. These were loaded into a buckboard driven by Sprague himself and, with Flinder leading the way on the roan mare, Molly, they jaunted out of Comas followed by the silence and the gloomy eyes of the people of the town.

# IV

## "ALONE IN THE BIG HOUSE"

They had come in the nick of time. Before the next morning the way up the pass from Comas would probably be impracticable for, when Flinder watched Sprague drive away through the early gloom of the winter afternoon, the south wind was freshening every moment and curling before it the wraith-like fingers of the coming snowstorm. Behind that curtain the proprietor's wagon soon disappeared, and Flinder set out upon a trip of exploration. He made the rounds of the sprawling array of buildings, carefully, noting everything with a particular eye.

Sprague Hotel, in the shape of a block U with stunted arms, faced south, looking upon the enormous shoulders and the lofty head of Comas Mountain. A little west of the main building were the stables and the outhouses of various sorts. The hotel stood on a low, broad-topped hill, the ground sloping rather rapidly away from it in all directions except the south, where a leveled stretch of meadow intervened before the abrupt rising of the hugest mountain in the entire range. Everywhere the big pines walked close and in dense ranks, save to the north where they were artificially thinned out to give a better view of the water of Lake Comas which curved in close to the side of the hotel. These waters were rapidly turning from blue to black as Flinder made his rounds, yet still they held a dim reflection of the snowy mountains which stood around it.

Lake Comas filled the bottom of a great pocket among the peaks and, around it, besides the overtowering mass of Comas Mountain and a receding host of lesser or more distant summits, sharp and numerous as waves raised by a storm wind and a cross tide, he numbered eight principal giants. South toward the far-off town rose Crane Mountain and Mount Warren, black against the last light of the day. To the north Hastings and Erskine and Druid Mountain bulked across the sky, while to the west a wild trio filled the horizon — Thunder Mountain, Justice Peak, and Old Misty, now justifying its name with a mass of the driving storm whipping away from its head like the hair of a racing mænad. In the south there was Mount Comas only and, compared with it, those eight monsters — each with a clothing of pine, each scarred by its own foaming streams, each rearing aloft a great white head — were like a circle of children gathered at the feet of the master to listen and never move for a million ages.

It was a true mountain pocket. A dozen little streams rushed down to Lake Comas with tributes of freshly iced waters, but there was no visible outlet. Through some narrow outlet under the lip of the lake the overflow sped away to appear again far beneath and pour through the plain near Comas town.

It was the thick of the dark before Flinder decided to return to the building and, as he went back through a narrow, black-throated avenue of pines with the wind striking against his face by jerks and starts, the eyes of a wild beast, two green spots of phosphorescent light, glared out at him around the edge of some shrubbery. He fired instantly. The creature faded noiselessly away. Flinder went on with a more sober spirit.

When he came under the building, there was still light enough to set the long rows of windows glimmering — ghostly spectators beholding him with dead eyes. What if there were living eyes at lurking watch behind them? He waited there for a moment, tasting the cold beginnings of fear with the peculiar relish of one to whom that emotion was a stranger. Over his head the wind was rushing louder every moment through the trees. Big as the hotel was, these ranks of forest monsters seemed ready to overwhelm it with a single forward stride.

He entered his quarters. Two rooms were set apart for his use. One was a little supplementary kitchen fitted up in the northern wing of the building. In it the food for the servants was prepared by a separate cook, for the talented individual who held sway in the main kitchen during the summer, pampering the delicate appetites of the guests, could not be expected to have a breakfast of ham and eggs and hot cakes and mush ready by seven or half-past six of a morning. Neither could he endure to have his domain invaded by some common camp cook. This snug kitchen, therefore, was reserved for the uses of the help, and now Flinder was installed in it. He had already lighted a fire in the stove, and the red tongues of the flames, glimmering through crevices here and there, faintly illumined the room. By that light he found the lantern and, when he had touched a match to the wick and lowered the chimney again, he set his hand on the knob of the adjoining door.

There he paused a moment, astonished at himself, for he found that he dreaded to advance into his own bedroom. Something scraped at the window of the kitchen. It must have been only a peculiar noise of the wind, but it made him jerk his head around and brought a damp perspiration out on his forehead. Twice he summoned his resolution, and twice he failed. At last he slipped the bale of the lantern over his left wrist, drew out his revolver, and gripping it so hard that it hurt the palm of his hand he cast the door open.

There was nothing but the empty room before him! He opened the closet — it was empty, save for the clothes which he had hung in it a few moments before. But still he was only half relieved. The cold weight lay in his heart even when he returned to the warmth of the kitchen. When he cooked his supper, his appetite, usually as voracious as that of a wild animal, had failed him. He found himself looking up every moment. Cold spasms seized the small of his back and made him jerk his head about to look wildly behind him; once he could have sworn that a definitely shaped shadow loomed beyond the window.

He drew the shade down quickly, but still he was not himself. When he washed the dishes, he found himself working with caution — as though in this lonely building in the wilderness there were danger that he might betray himself to the hearing of another living creature! Again and again he paused with lifted head and straining eyes to listen.

He was weak when he finished. He opened the fire door to the stove. The outpouring of the red light and the blasting heat was to Flinder like the voice of a friend. It wakened his mind to such a point that he could at least argue the matter with himself.

Something was wrong. Of that he had no doubt. From some direction danger was pointing toward him. He added up the possibilities. It might be that friends of Ormond, of Denny, or of Hugh Kirk had ridden up from Comas to revenge their injured comrades upon the person of him who had struck the three down in a single night. It might be that word had gone forth to the Lewis brothers that their sworn enemy was now alone among their own mountains.

Yet surely it would take a hot soul of revenge to weather such a storm as this and bring the warriors with frozen hands and numbed brains to the work of attacking such a man as Ben Flinder. The wind had risen suddenly and was still rising. There were mutterings, roarings, sudden wrenchings of the blast as it worked in anger at the big hotel, while all the time a small voice screamed in the heart of the sky, a dreadful, threatening overtone. Sometimes, when the voice of the wind lessened, he could hear the sheeted masses of the driven snow striking against the wall and the window with a strangely muffled sound, like the soft beating of the wings of a monstrous moth. Sometimes there was a small musketry of sleet whipped against the hotel.

30

No, surely his enemies would not venture out against him through the heart of such a storm. Yet there was danger near; he could have sworn it. But wherein could it be?

One thought came to him at last. He was used to the wilderness, but it was the wilderness of open skies or a hasty little lean-to against a mountainside or a great tree — shelters which kept him on the border of the storm and not out of it. But this great building was made for many voices of many men, and laughter and stomping, and whiskey in front of the fire. He drew out his own flask but corked it again, untasted. He had no heart, it seemed, to drink alone.

In the meantime one of his tasks waited for him. He had promised old Thomas Sprague one thing, and one thing only — that twice each day he would make the rounds of the buildings on the outside and see that all was well, and that once by day and once by night he would go through every chamber of the hotel to see that all was well. The time for that night inspection had come. He told himself frankly that, if he waited for another five minutes, it would be impossible for him to force himself through the empty, storm-echoing halls of the place.

Even now, it was only by telling himself that he was turning coward that he was able to rouse his spirits. First he trimmed the lantern's wick of a rough corner, and then he turned it up until it gave the maximum flame without smoking. Next he slipped off his boots and put upon his feet silent moccasins of soft thick elk hide. Then, with his lantern bail hooked over his left arm to leave the left hand free for turning doorknobs and with the old Colt firmly in his right hand, he began the tour.

To leave the kitchen was like leaving a circle of friends. He shivered an instant in the long hall, then he went on, opening the doors on either side, holding the lantern high for a glance within. Sometimes the light flared back at him from a mirror's face like a bull's-eye opened against his face. Sometimes it rippled

31

along the naked springs of a bed, for the bedding, even the mat-tresses, had been securely stored against the damp of the winter. But in every room there was something to startle him.

He grew furious at his own timidity. Once he made himself clear his throat with a loud noise. A long, dreary echo answered him down the hall, and he waited, awestruck, until it died. Then, his face cold with perspiration, he raised a whistle. He could not tell what tune it was or what the key. But he made a noise — an eerie companion during that tour of inspection.

The lower floor completed, having passed through the long dining room and the parlors, there remained the harder ordeal of the second story. The stairs muttered and squeaked like run-ning rats beneath his feet. The very first door he opened gave him a blast of wind that knocked the flame high in the throat of the chimney and then set it flickering and dying. He turned aside until the flame had regained its strength. Then, his teeth set, sheltering the lantern behind him and with the great shadow of his body leaning before, he forced himself through the doorway. That room was empty, but the window had been left a trifling inch ajar and through it enough snow had blown already to film the floor with white. He made the window fast and, after that last shock, the rest of the night journey was simple enough.

When he returned to the kitchen, it was like stepping back into the presence of kind, familiar faces. He sat down, breathing hard, and opened the damper of the stove until the fire roared, and the chimney stack began to redden half way to the ceiling. Even so, though the room was stifling, it did not give him the sort of inward warmth which he needed.

He went to the bedroom. Once inside he examined it carefully. He opened the closet a second time. At last, red with shame though there was no eye to behold him, he kneeled and looked under the bed. But still his nerves were quivering when he went back into the kitchen again.

32

He had hardly seated himself when he heard a scratching such as had come before at the window, but this time at the door. The wind dropped at that moment to a far-off murmuring, and very clearly he distinguished the sniffing of a beast along the crack at the bottom of the door.

A load of inexpressible weight was lifted from his heart. A mere beast — neither man nor ghost, then, had been oppressing him with its nearness — the same, no doubt, at which he had fired earlier in the evening. Perhaps the odor of the cooking food had attracted it from the starved wilderness with the beginning of the snows. If he were quick enough now, he could put a bullet into it. At least he could frighten it out of its curiosity forever. Stealing to the door, his gun ready, Flinder thrust it open with a sudden shout. There was no frightened whine, no lightning retreat. At his feet crouched a white monster with mouth snarled open and glittering green eyes.

# V

## "THE GRAY SHADOW"

Flinder, as he leaped back, slipped to his knees and, firing at the same time, knew as he pulled the trigger that he had missed. Springing after him, the mantle of snow dropped from the back of the forest creature. It was a great lobo that flung at him, aimed straight at his throat. The fall which made Flinder's bullet go wide nevertheless saved his life. The wolf slash that might have torn his throat out struck his head instead. It was like the blow of a club and the rip of a knife combined, but the sting of the wound acted like a spur and brought him to his full strength.

It was like a horror out of a fairy tale, this attack by a wild beast on a man in his own house, but at least here was no werewolf, no bodiless terror. Flinder's revolver had fallen to the floor. He had no time to scoop it up again, but wheeling about he met the next rush of the great loafer with his long arms thrust out. He caught the throat of the snarling devil just beneath the head, and his strong arms fended off the gnashing teeth, but the shock toppled him backward on the floor, rolled him over. Now the struggling body of the monster was between his legs, and his gripping fingers were working deeper into the throat of the wolf.

Only the very blindness of blind luck had given him that hold. Had it fallen but an inch lower, his forearms would have been cut to ribbons in a trice, but his grip was so close to the head that its motions were impeded. Even so the great, white fangs ripped the sleeve of his coat away and grazed the skin, cutting like a knife.

There were a hundred and fifty pounds of that giant of the mountains, a hundred and fifty pounds of gaunt muscle and bone and, if he gained an inch of freedom, Flinder knew that his last minute on earth had come. He drove his grip deeper. The long tongue of the wolf began to loll out; his eyes reddened and seemed bursting from his head. To Flinder it seemed as though he were playing the part of a child holding down the full strength of a man by a trick hold.

A convulsive effort nearly broke his hold. He jammed the Gray Shadow — for he had no doubt that this was that same cruel hunter — into a corner of the room and exerted the last power of his grip. Under it the loafer, biting at the air, shuddered strongly and then lay still. When Flinder released his grip and sprang back to get his gun, the big animal simply rolled limply upon his side.

He was not dead but throttled out of its wind for the moment. The long hind legs still twitched a little and their movements

34

grew stronger — the lungs of the brute began to labor, and Flinder pressed the muzzle of the Colt against the ear of the lobo. Twice his forefinger tightened, and twice it relaxed on the trigger. A foolish thought had come to him that here, after all, was company in his time of loneliness, a devilish company, to be sure, but better the fiend himself as an associate than the long, listening hours of this building. He took a length of light steel chain, fastened it around the neck of the beast, dragged the burden into a corner, and spiked the chain against the wall. He had barely driven the long nails home when the loafer recovered enough life to rip at him as he leaped back.

Leaving his prisoner there, he looked to himself. The mirror showed him a wonderful picture of a face covered with crimson, his hair a tangle of clotted red, his sleeves in ribbons from the snapping teeth of the great animal, his trousers in shreds, and his legs scratched in a hundred places by the flying claws of the wolf. He looked like something which had passed through a mill.

When the cut in his head was washed, it proved neither long nor deep, and the bleeding stopped of itself. As for his clothes, the generosity of Thomas Sprague had provided him amply. In the bedroom he togged himself forth anew and returned to the kitchen.

A throat-tearing snarl greeted him. The Gray Shadow crouched on his belly and leaped forward — the strong chain, as he flew through mid-air, snapped him down against the floor like the cracker on the end of a whiplash. The stunning blow stretched him senseless for an instant, but presently he staggered to his feet again, snarling as before, then backed into a corner and snapped at the bond which held him. The steel links clashed under the stroke.

There could be no doubt that this was the Gray Shadow. Along one haunch there was a red furrow; that was where the bullet

35

must have marked the beast earlier in the day. Flinder, his hair bristling with astonishment and horror, sat down to consider the giant, not so much the great body as the wise and evil brain which had enabled the wolf to trail the man who had wounded him across Comas and up the twisting miles of the trail until the man "went to earth," so to speak. It reminded him of certain uncanny tales of grizzly bears which he had heard from old hunters.

He studied the frame of the killer. The more he regarded the Gray Shadow the more he was convinced that the townsfolk were right. Dog and wolf must have been crossed to achieve this result, some king among the loafer wolves with a great-thewed, wise-headed Saint Bernard perhaps. The ears were shorter and broader than in most lobos. The pale gray of the belly and the darker gray of the sides turned to a saddle of brown across the back. The loafer slopes from gigantic shoulders to dwindling hind quarters, almost like a hyena, but this animal was built as nobly behind as before. Above all, there was a silken expanse of white hair upon the chest of the brute. If it was the wolf in the creature that made it so savage, it was the dog element that gave it courage so boldly to hunt man.

The Gray Shadow, having proved to his satisfaction that the slender steel links of the chain were nevertheless mysteriously stronger than his big teeth, drew back into the corner, lay down and, raising his great head, stared calmly at his conqueror. It was the quiet of consuming hatred and malice, cruel and deadly and unforgiving.

That night, though Flinder left the door between kitchen and bedroom open, there was not a sound from the prisoner to disturb his light sleep. When he wakened the next morning, he found himself in a new world. The sky was still dark with solid clouds. The wind had fallen much from the height of the storm, but it still carried white pencilings of snow. All the mountains were muffled in white which covered every open stretch, buried the streams from sight, and loaded the branches of the big evergreens with level strokes of brilliant white. He waded around the building for his morning inspection through drifts knee deep. Then he returned to the kitchen and the Gray Shadow.

As for the terrors of the night before, now that the day had come, they seemed obscure and distant follies. Yet he was glad of even this companion when he stepped through the door, and the wolf dog rose, immense, before him. The beast indulged in no foolish threats, not a growl, not a snarl, not a baring of the white teeth, but with self-contained dignity it watched and waited.

Only when breakfast was cooking did he prick his ears, and his eyes grew bright with yearning at the smell of food. Watching the saliva drool from his mouth, Flinder had an idea and chuckled brutally over it. Famine might make this forest rover as gentle and as helpless as a child. Not famine of food alone, for that would require days and days to a belly used to starvation, but famine of water also which breaks body and spirit almost at a stroke. In the heat of the kitchen, blanketed under that thick pelt, the work would go on apace. Indeed, before mid-morning the tongue of the monster was lolling out and, at noon, the patience was gone from his eyes. By mid-afternoon he was a snarling, mad-eyed picture of desperation, his eyes fixed longingly out the window at the world of cold, white snow. Before night fell, he was trembling with fever and with weakness.

Flinder, coming back from his moccasined tour of the building in the first dark of the night, found the Gray Shadow walking back and forth with uncertain steps, swaying at the limits of his chain. He gave him a silent curling of the lip with the great fangs yawning open, but Flinder laughed and walked on to the bedroom. What was pain to him? He had passed through his hell. Let the rest of the world share in turn.

Twice he wakened that night and heard a hoarse sound of panting from the kitchen. He fell asleep again each time to dream that the gray prison wall rose around him once more and that the stripes clothed his body and that his view of life was crossed by strong steel bars. He wakened in a savage mood.

When he entered the kitchen, the Gray Shadow rose, swayed feebly on his legs, and sank down again. His eyes were a dull red; a cracked and swollen tongue protruded from his mouth. When Flinder cooked his breakfast, there was no stir, no light of hunger in the wolf's eyes. Compared with the torment of thirst, the craving for food had become a mere nothing. That afternoon Flinder threw bread on the floor beside the poor brute. The food lay untouched, and he knew that his time had come now to make the experiment.

With his revolver leveled in a steady hand, he advanced within the circle of the chain. The Gray Shadow lifted its head and glared. He stretched out his hand. The Gray Shadow bared his great fangs — then dropped his head again to the floor. He was beaten thoroughly in body and soul! Only the harsh sound of his breathing went on and the ceaseless roving of his eyes from side to side which showed that madness was coming. Flinder sat down cross-legged beside the helpless giant and talked to him, while he ran his fingers through the coarse outer hair of the pelt and into the thick, warm underfur.

"Here's the two of us," said Flinder in his deep, rough voice. "Here's you, old-timer, too much dog to keep away from menfolks, and too darn much wolf to make friends with 'em. That's me, too. I can't live without 'em. And, by heaven, how I hate 'em when I'm near! Now, loafer, you've killed men's hosses . . . you've murdered their cows. You've tried to butcher even a man . . . that's me. Why in the devil don't I put a bullet through you . . . and keep nothin' but your hide to remember you by?"

He put his hand under the jaw of the Gray Shadow. There was a harsh growl, and the ready lips twitched back to show the glistening fangs. But under the steady eyes of the man the eyes of the brute fell.

"That's why," muttered Flinder. "They beat me by a trick. They got me where they could throw me into a dark cell and leave me there till I was willing to give in . . . till I was willing to promise to be good." He waited as he remembered that humiliation. "And I'm beatin' you by a trick, too. But the minute I give you water, you'll be ready to knife me with them teeth. I know your black heart, you devil! Well . . . we'll try."

He went to the sink at the farther side of the room. There he filled a washbasin with water and brought it back. The very sound of the running water had brought the Gray Shadow slavering to the end of his chain, and the moment the basin was on the floor his nose was in it, lapping it up in great mouthfuls, quivering with joy.

Flinder kept one hand on the edge of the basin while the brute drank. One hand was there, and the other presented the black muzzle of the revolver. He risked a hand ruined for life. Nevertheless the thrill of the long gambling chance made him take it. He saw the water disappear. Then the Gray Shadow lifted his head, mad with hunger for more and, looking into the face of the man, a shudder ran through his body, a new and wistful light came into his eyes, and in his great throat a sound which had never been there before — the whine of a dog!

Flinder gaped upon him. Still all at sea with amazement, he brought a second basin and as the great animal lapped at it — behold a second marvel. His tail began to wag — that true sign of a dog's gratitude and joy. He drank half that basin, scattering the water over the floor with every lap of his long tongue. Then content, he stretched himself on his belly and licked the man's hand upon the basin — he who had inflicted the torment and

39

then chosen to end it.

Flinder was overcome. "Partner," he said huskily, "there's good even in you. But what about me? What about me?"

# VI

## "A FUGITIVE?"

Life at the hotel had become endurable but far from pleasant since the coming of the Gray Shadow. The tours of the grounds and the building by day were mere nothings. But that trip through the whispering halls and the living shadows by night was a dreadful ordeal still. It made no difference that Flinder told himself all was folly; it made no difference that he cursed himself as a coward. In fact, there was real danger, both from the direction of the town of Comas and from these mountains where the Lewis brothers were sure to have learned by this time that their deadly enemy was living here alone and exposed to them. But the dread of men was not in Flinder. It was the empty silence of the big place. It was the horror of pushing open door after door in the night, never knowing what might be found inside. He could have made the round a hundred times, he told himself, without having a shred of that terror diminish. Each night he told himself that his luck had been used up, and that now was the time for some unearthly calamity to fall upon him.

Another melancholy idea came to him shortly after — that it was vitally and cruelly wrong of him to pen up the Gray Shadow in this narrow den when the right of the animal was the wilderness to hunt in and die in when his time came. So on the seventh morning he loosed the chain and opened the door. The hasty pads of the Gray Shadow scratched and slipped on the floor, then the wolf dog hurtled out into the open.

Ben Flinder, from the doorway with the wind cutting at his face, sadly watched the big beast strike a fluffy drift of snow, roll in it, spring to his feet biting and snarling at flying bits of the stuff, and then dart off under the trees. He had heard of how wild beasts, being tamed, would return to those who had come to love them. He knew now what a void there would be in his heart when the great brute was gone forever. And the Gray Shadow had no heed of the man behind him. He rushed away into the forest. For a cold half hour Ben Flinder waited at the door, but there was no sign of a return. There had not been so much as a backward glance at him.

"I should have sunk a chunk of lead in him and skinned him," Flinder told himself gloomily.

He went back to the work of washing the breakfast dishes. To be alone now, having grown used to companionship, was worse than before. In vain he made half a dozen rounds of the outer buildings during the day to keep his mind employed. In vain he went down to the lake from whose surface the wind had burnished away the snow. Lake Comas was a solid face of ice, inches thick. The wind had shaken the snow out of the pines, but the ground was everywhere piled deep with it, drift upon drift which would be buried deep and deeper as the winter grew old and which would not melt until the heat of the late spring days began. Coming back up the slope, a mink, furious on a blood trail, darted across his path, almost under his feet. It crouched before the shadow of his coming, opened to him a mouth filled with little needle teeth, and then darted away among the underbrush. Winter certainly had come. And if it began so gloomily, what would be his state of mind before the season had ended?

When he returned to the kitchen that evening, the first thing that his eye fell upon was the chain which had fastened the Gray Shadow, lying in a bright, snaky coil in the corner. He put it

41

away hastily, with a little touch of bitterness. For there, he told himself, had been the one thing in the world which he could love.

He had made a foolish compromise between himself and the letter of his promise which was that, instead of waiting for the full dark before he began his tour of the building, he went about it after the sun was down, but before the brief winter twilight had thickened to night.

This evening, however, when he returned, the fire was out in the kitchen stove, and a fire there was most necessary. The temperature had fallen ten or fifteen degrees during the day with a north wind rising every moment and sending small fingers of icy cold through every crevice in the walls of the hotel. By the time he had removed the ashes and built up a strong fire, the dark was upon him and, looking at the black well of the window-pane with the yellow reflection from the lamp far in its depths, he mused gloomily for a moment, half deciding that he would postpone that evening's inspection trip.

It was not conscience which kept him to his promise. It was the bitter shame of his own cowardice. So, with lantern and gun, he began his trip, pushing his unwilling self down the lower corridor, opening door after door, then climbing the noisy staircase while the wind howled and laughed fiendishly outside the building. Down the upper hall he passed, still opening doors right and left, still with his heart tightening at every step. Once he paused to moisten his dry lips. If the Gray Shadow were only waiting for his return in the kitchen, how much easier it would be.

A quarter of his work still remained. He stepped to the next door, cast it open and, as the lantern light swept in a wave through the chamber, a wild voice shrieked and died in mid-stream as though a hand had been clapped over the parted lips. Flinder shrank back with bristling hair. He cast a glance behind him,

42

and the long hall seemed hardly less terrible to flee along than the black doorway before him. So he ran straightforward into the room. There was nothing before him! The whole chamber was empty. He looked with a sort of feverish hope toward the window. The sill was heaped high up the pane with undisturbed snow. No one could have fled by that opening even had it been possible to climb through it in the brief interval since he had heard the cry. The closet, likewise, was empty. He hurried around behind the bed, and then he stumbled over a soft body on the floor.

What restrained him from shooting instantly he never knew. Swinging the lantern forward as he recovered himself and turned, he saw the white, emaciated face of a girl with closed eyes, her arms thrown out crosswise in the posture of her fall. She was not dead, though the thin face, purple with cold, looked like death indeed. That scream, then, had been the cry of her terror when she saw the flooding light of the lantern and saw Flinder behind it.

How could she have come here? When could she have come? Why was she there? Who had brought her, considering that such a slender creature could hardly have ventured through the wilderness of this winter day with the snow driving before the wind.

He lifted her in his arms — how easily she lay there with the lightness of a child, her head hanging limply down. He shifted her so that her head fell against his shoulder, and her cold face was against his neck as he carried her down the hall and down the stairs hastily. Then it seemed to Flinder that she was not breathing, and he bolted in a blind panic for the kitchen.

He laid her on the floor close to the stove. He tore the gloves from her hands. The thin fingers were blue with cold, and he thought for a moment that fear and exposure together had broken her heart. Helplessly chafing the icy hands, he stared into her face. It was exquisitely made. The mouth, with the delicate faded

43

purple of the lips, was a thing to marvel over, and the great eyes were shadowed over with exhaustion. The brow was like the very marble of death, and nothing lived about her saving the masses of black hair, shivering in the draught which swept along the floor.

He plunged into the bedroom and, returning, wrapped her in armfuls of blankets. At the same moment her eyes opened and strained at his face as though striving and dreading to recognize in him something which she feared.

"You're not one of them," she breathed. "Oh, thank heaven! But you're one of their men. Are they coming? When will they be here?" She cast the blankets away and swayed to her feet.

"I'm my own man," said Flinder frowning. "Where are you goin'?"

She had started for the outer door when he stepped before her. At that she shrank from him in such terror that it made Ben Flinder swallow hard.

"You ain't goin' to keep me?" she cried out to him.

"D'you want to go out and die in the snow?" he asked her roughly. "Hell and fire, girl, in them clothes you'd last five minutes. No more."

"I've never harmed *you*," she began to moan. "I don't aim to do you no harm. I only want to get away. If I stay, they'll find me!"

"Who's they?"

She did not hear him, or hearing she did not understand. "They're comin' now. They're comin' now! Listen!"

She stared at him with wild eyes, pointing at the door. Ben Flinder, listening, heard a scratching at the door.

"Partner?" he called.

In reply a long, wailing cry of a wolf rang behind the door. The last note was drowned in the scream of the girl.

"They're here!"

"Who?" cried Flinder.

"Wolves!" cried the girl. "They've come for me. Will you let them take me? Will you . . . ?"

Clinging to him, her head went suddenly back, and she would have collapsed on the floor had it not been for the sweeping arm of Flinder. Carrying her thus easily in the capacious hold of one strong arm, he went to the door and threw it open.

The Gray Shadow slid past him into the center of the room. As Flinder closed the door, the brute sighted the form of the girl and crouched on his belly with a murderous snarl. He had hunted well and fed that day. His gaunt flanks were filled out, but the wolf famine which never dies was in his look now.

"You murderin' devil!" growled out Ben Flinder. "Get back!"

The Gray Shadow rewarded him with a wicked snarl, but nevertheless he shrank back into his old corner where the chain had lain before and, sitting there, he cocked his head upon one side and wrinkled his forehead as he stared at the master.

# VII

## "RIGHTS AND WRONGS NO MATTER"

Ben had two fears. The one was lest those from whom the girl was flying should overtake her in this place. The other was lest the wolf dog might come at her.

She lay in his bed in a delirium half that night, raving and tossing and sometimes striving to rise from the bed and run out into the dark of the storm, crying out that they were coming now, that she heard their voices in the wind — that wild wind which was shouting around the house and shaking it in a strong grip. While he kept her safe and covered warm, the Gray Shadow

45

stood in the open kitchen door and snarled at the girl like a very devil.

Sometimes, in that strange night, it seemed to Ben Flinder that the wolf dog with uncanny prescience was foreseeing a danger that the girl would bring upon them both. Again he laid the fury of the Gray Shadow to the sheer wickedness of that hunter of flesh or, at most, to jealousy because the master paid so much heed to another and so little to him. For whenever Flinder stepped from the bedroom into the kitchen, the Gray Shadow fawned on him with whinings like a dog that welcomes a long-absent master.

The girl grew quieter in the dogwatch of the night. At that time he was able to make her eat crackers soaked in a rich broth. He had to feed her like a child and, with the blank, unseeing eyes of an infant, she watched the spoon and then his face. After that, her head in the pillow and the red mist of delirium clearing from her mind, she stared at him with a troubled frown that grew less and less until her hand closed over his with a faint pressure, and she fell asleep.

Now for the first time he could really see her since her eyes were closed. He could study her little by little. She was younger, much younger than she had seemed at first. That was very clear. She could not be more, he felt, than eighteen or nineteen years old at the most, and she was less than that in her thoughts. Her hand was the hand of a woman, but her throat was the throat of a child. Now in her sleep a sob rose, and a tear welled up through the thick, dark lashes that lay against her cheek.

Ben Flinder, terribly moved, glared about him. If he could have found, at that moment, those who were the cause of this sorrow even in the girl's sleep, their shrift would have been short indeed. He leaned a little over her, and at this the faintest of smiles came upon her lips, trembling to life, dying again, and living once more like a ghost of gentle happiness in her face.

46

It seemed to Ben Flinder that the smile came at the very moment that his shadow brushed across her. At least that thought came warmly home to him, and he pondered it slowly.

What had come over him he hardly knew. It was strange in his life. It was a queer happiness that was half sadness, something that made his heart ache and his lips smile, as though from a cold, dark cell and through a barred window he were looking out on a sun-flooded day of April. He went back into the kitchen again. The Gray Shadow greeted him with a malevolent and silent baring of the fangs while his mane bristled, but Flinder was beginning to have an insight into the workings of that wild brain. He spoke quietly to the wolf dog and, going up to the monster without fear, he saw the flattened ears prick suddenly, the great head with its wrinkled brow of wisdom turned to one side to listen to this gentle human voice, and suddenly the Gray Shadow had reared and, with his forepaws large as a man's hands on the shoulders of Flinder, he licked the face of his master.

"You been jealous," muttered Flinder as he extricated himself and wiped his face. "Damned me if you ain't been jealous, you old fool!"

A faint cry from the bedroom brought him hastily back to the girl. She was turning and twisting in the bed and, by the dim light from the kitchen lamp that shone through the doorway, he saw that her face was troubled. When he sat down by her and spoke softly, the darkness disappeared. The Gray Shadow snarled savagely from the door and brought an answering moan of terror from the delirious sleep of the girl. Flinder looked about him in dismay, but seeing that there was only one way out of his difficulty, he brought the Gray Shadow into the chamber and tied him securely to his own leg.

The moment he was sitting by her again, the girl dropped into a smiling slumber, and Flinder brooded above her with the same swelling heart of happiness. It was as though he had taken her soul into his hand to give it shelter. And she, too, had taken hold upon him. If she sighed, a tremor ran through him. If she smiled in her slumber, he smiled in turn. It was too strange for analysis. He could find only one analogy and that was out of his childhood when he read in a fairy tale how the prince came into the enchanted castle where a thousand perils slept around him and so reached the treasure chamber, flooded with rubies rich as blood, and sea-green emeralds, and the crystal light of diamonds.

Many a time, in spirit, he had stood within the iron bars of the treasure room beside the brave young prince, where a king's wealth could have been cupped in the palm of one hand. So he felt now as he watched the girl. There was the same thrill along the blood, the same ecstasy of spirit, the same sense of perilous unreality.

The Gray Shadow was performing most strangely. First he had sneaked as close to the bed as the carefully held rope permitted, his lips writhed silently back from his teeth, his eyes filled with the green light of devilish malice. For long moments he held that position, then he curled suddenly at the feet of his master and went to sleep, as though he had looked to the bottom of this matter and found that the creature was not worthy of his jealousy.

Flinder presently found himself nodding, too. He slept wretchedly by fits and starts. The fire had died down in the kitchen but, though he had energy enough to pile fresh covers on the bed, he did not have enough wide-awake resolution to build up the fire in the stove. He sat shivering and shuddering in the chair, his chin fallen upon his breast. Sometimes in a lucid interval he glanced at the girl and wondered at the smiling peace upon her face. Once, when he wakened, he saw that the monster wolf dog had risen from his place so softly that the master had not been disturbed and had approached the sleeper, for what

48

fiendish purpose could only be guessed. Or perhaps it was only to look again and to wonder, for when Flinder saw him, the great, scarred head of the Gray Shadow dropped upon the bed and, with pricking ears, he watched silently the marble face of the girl, short inches from his muzzle. More than that! She had thrown out her arm carelessly in her sleep, and one delicately slender hand lay on the head of the beast, half lost in the gray, deep fur. There was no need of further proof for Flinder. There was enchantment in this girl, and even with the Gray Shadow she was safe. At that the unconscious guard which he had been keeping upon the room was lost, and he dropped into a heavy sleep.

When he wakened, a bright shaft of winter sunlight had struck through the window and was flaming on the wall nearby. He turned his head down to where the Gray Shadow should have been. The beast was not there! Neither had he chewed the slender rope in two with quietly gnawing teeth, for no fragment of the rope remained. It had been untied. He glanced to the bed. It was empty! The clothes had been turned back over the foot of the bed. The girl, too, was gone. As he started up, a laughing vision stood before him in the kitchen doorway, shielding her eyes from the glare of the white sun.

It was she! But, ah, how changed from the cold and half-dying creature of the night before. A rich color lived in her cheeks, a rich life in her eyes, and such a smile was shining down at him that Flinder thought half the world must feel it and come to take her from him.

"Poor fellow," she was saying. "Are you near dead with the cold? Come on into the kitchen and get warm. The coffee is pretty close to ready. Smell it?"

He wandered into the kitchen with vague eyes, with fumbling feet, with a brain benumbed and, standing with his hands spread out over the heat of the stove, he watched her hurrying back and forth. He was not the only spectator. The Gray Shadow, the terrible and man-slaying Gray Shadow, roved here and there behind her, his eyes never shifting from her face, his great claws scuttling noisily across the floor.

"Here," she panted at last. "I thought it would never boil. There isn't anything as provoking as a coffee pot, is there?"

She poured the coffee. She set his cup on the table where two places were laid on opposite sides. How neatly all was furnished forth. There was ham fried until the edges of the slices were a crisped brown, a miracle of the frying pan which Flinder had never been able to achieve. There were potatoes browned to a turn. There was this enchanting aroma of coffee in the air; a glass of red strawberry jam shone resplendent on the table.

And now: "Here's a surprise!" she said. "You haven't had these for a while, I guess. Get out of my way, silly dog!"

Behold, she flicked the Gray Shadow out of her way with a single gesture of that light hand of hers, and the brute followed, grinning, with his red tongue hanging out, while she wrenched open the oven door. Forth poured the indescribably comforting fragrance of baked bread, and then a great pan of white bellied, yellow-crusted biscuits was brought forth and held high with the girl laughing beneath it.

"They look fine," was all Ben Flinder could find to say.

One could wish to say that food was as nothing in the eyes of Ben Flinder, and that to feast his eyes upon the picture of his visitor he could forget all matters less than those of the spirit, but being an analyst of truth, that broad and common truth must be admitted. At the first taste of that coffee — how different from the black and shining lye that he made for himself! — he forgot all things save his material man.

How he ate upon this morning it would be an Homeric task to relate for, after ten years of prison diet sauced with black looks, it seemed to him that he was eating food for the first time since his boyhood. When at last the plates were emptied, he sighed and looked up at her. How long before she had finished her own repast he could not guess, but now, with her soft, bared elbows resting on the edge of the table and with her fists tucked under her chin, she was watching him with a peculiar smile of maternal happiness and amusement. Ben Flinder felt suddenly very young. He blushed and grinned at the same moment.

"D'you feel better?' she asked him.

"A heap," said Ben Flinder. "And. . . ." He looked about him to find something to say, and his glance rested on the Gray Shadow, who sat beside the table with his eyes fixed steadily on the face of the girl. "What did you do to that dog?" he asked. "How'd you tame him?"

"Oh," said the girl, "he's a kind old thing. When I got up, he began to whine for me, and I was afraid that he'd wake you up, so I untied him and took him along."

He sighed again. But, after all, miracles must be a common event in her life.

"And how could you cook all this without making a noise?"

"I couldn't. You snored loud enough to cover the racket."

They laughed together but stopped in the same instant as the wind, which had been droning in the distance, leaped down on the building and struck it with a great hand. They listened afterward. A shutter began to bang far off. —

"First," said Ben Flinder, automatically lowering his voice, "tell me how you come here?"

She frowned wistfully at him. He saw her lips part. Then they closed again, and she shook her head.

"I can't tell you that."

"Nor your name?" asked Flinder.

"I . . . my name is Mary."

"Is that all you can say?"

"That's all."

51

She was beginning to dread him and shrink.

"My name is Ben Flinder," he said. "Does that mean anything to you?"

"It means that you saved me last night from dyin' of the cold, Ben Flinder."

He could not help but breathe deeply with relief. Better, far better, that his past should be buried from her.

"Last night you was scared," he said. "You thought something was follerin' you. Are you still afraid of that?"

"Yes. If they can track me."

He took her to the door and opened it a little so that they could both look out. The wind was sweeping low-brushing clouds of snow along the ground.

"Would tracks stay in that sort of snow?" he asked her.

"I don't know," said the girl. "But he . . . they . . . they could track me through anything, I guess."

He slammed the door and turned on her. "How?" he asked sharply.

She shrugged her shoulders helplessly. "I don't know," she said, while her eyes read his face, as though hunting for comfort there. "How do buzzards know where to fly?"

"It sounds queer," said Ben Flinder. "There ain't many men could walk through that sort of weather, let alone foller a trail. Tell me this much . . . have you done something wrong?"

"Yes," she whispered.

"Have they got a right to take you back with them if they find you?"

She was backing away from him. "Yes," she said even more faintly.

Ben Flinder stamped upon the floor so that the whole room shook, and the Gray Shadow snarled in startled surprise.

"Rights and wrongs don't make no difference to me," he said. "If you want to stay here, Mary, I'll keep you as long as I can."

# VIII

## "THE HOTEL AFIRE"

That fervid declaration brought a smile to her lips, but it seemed to Ben Flinder that even as she thanked him a deep gleam was gathering in her eyes. She gathered the dishes and began to wash them at the sink, but ever and again her hands grew idle, the clinking half muffled beneath the water ceased, and he would look up to see her dreaming at the frost-whitened face of the window before her. The heart of Ben Flinder swelled as he watched. It was worse than prison. For here his hands were free and only his ignorance could keep him from doing what he wanted to do, and that was to help her and to defend her with all his strength. He strode before her.

"Mary," he said, "open up to me and tell me the whole damned mess. I'll show you the way. I'll tell you about myself. They put me in prison for ten years for murder. Then they found out that they was wrong. Well, Mary, you can build on the top of that and make out how much I think of their laws. Tell me the whole story."

She straightened from the sink and so doing her head came just to the hollow of his shoulder. Bending back a little until she touched him, she looked up to his face, smiling slightly but very sober, as he could see.

"I can't tell you a thing," she said. "God bless you for wanting to help. But I can't tell you a thing. That'd make you to blame, too."

"Make me to blame for what? Mary, I can't see that there ain't no way that you could really do anything wrong. You ain't made for that."

She rested against him, looking up at him with a sad and quiet curiosity. Then she shook her head again.

"You don't know," she said. Fire flashed up in her. She turned sharply upon him. "I tell you, Ben, I've wanted to do murder . . . murder!"

Here she stopped, catching her breath and staring at him with a sudden terror as though she dreaded lest he had been able to look through into her mind. She turned back to her dishes.

Ben Flinder began to pace the floor. There was such a confusion of surmise and fear in his mind that for a time he was utterly unable to speak to her, but afterward he drew close again. He placed a huge hand on the edge of the sink and leaned beside her, watching her hands dabbling idly in the steaming water at the dishes clouded over with suds.

"Mary," he cried, "tell me the truth about it. I guess what's happened. I see the whole thing. Dog-gone me if I ain't a fool to not have guessed right off. You . . . you up and got rid of that man that was botherin' you. You . . . you killed him, Mary! Is that it? Say it out. God knows that I wouldn't blame you none!"

"Not that," she answered. "But I almost wish that I'd done it."

He saw her on the trembling verge of tears, but his eagerness to get at the heart of the thing made him brutal. He took her by both shoulders. He even shook her a little in the vehemence of his passion.

"Tell me just this one thing. Tell me if this man . . . if he's your husband, Mary, or just someone who has been unkind to you."

As for Mary, her only answer was a burst of tears. Ben Flinder was so unnerved that he ran for the door, pausing neither for hat nor coat, and ran out into the storm.

He rushed straight against it, while his hair clotted with snow, and the weight of the wind burned his face. He rushed into the sweep of snow, knee-deep, and found a fierce satisfaction in wasting his strength against the elements. When his breath began to fail, he turned back.

It was a cold, wet return journey. Half way to the hotel a white monster rushed at him and then swept in a circle about him, whining with joy. It was the Gray Shadow. They went back together and, together, when he had brushed off the snow as well as he could, they entered the kitchen again. He found Mary, white-faced, her hands clasped together. Such a radiance came into her eyes as he strode through the door, that he marveled at her.

"What did you hear? What was it?" she cried to him. "I was half mad . . . seeing you run out like that. I thought . . . God knows what! Then I sent the dog out. I thought if there were danger, he might help. . . ."

He had not intended any brutal discourtesy, but this was too much for him to face. He felt that he could not stand before her for another five minutes without letting her look into him as clearly as though his heart had been a transparent thing. So he strode across the kitchen without a word and passed into the corridor. He came back in time to find her huddling her cloak about her shoulders, turning the broad collar over her head, and moving toward the door as she did so. He stopped her with a sharp word.

"I'm just going out . . . ," said a stifled voice, and she did not turn toward him.

"For what?" he growled out.

"For . . . wood . . . the fire, you see. . . ."

"I'll bring the wood we need."

"Besides . . . I want a walk. . . ."

"Hell and fire!" thundered Ben Flinder. "You couldn't stand to that wind for half a minute!" He blocked the door before her. Then he saw that the tears were running fast down her

55

face. "What is it, Mary?" he asked more gently.

"Nothin'," said the girl. "Except I see. . . ."

"What?"

"You don't want me here, Ben Flinder."

He stamped, and the water flew from his wet boot. "I'll tell you what," he said. "It'll take more'n two men to get you away. Are you stronger than two men, Mary?"

She put up her head at that, filled with some emotion stronger than shame for her tears and, going to him, she took his hands and looked fairly into his face. She looked at him a little bewildered, and so he left her quickly, because his heart was too full to let him stay near her another moment. He roved through the hours restlessly. Where was his dread of the long halls and the empty chambers and the howling wind outside? It was all gone. It seemed a far younger and more foolish man had trembled at these little things before.

He came down, changed his clothes, and went out to make the rounds of the building. Through the day he made it his business to find as much as possible to do outside the hotel. As he walked, he turned the matter ceaselessly back and forth through his mind. In some manner he must draw the entire truth from her.

When the evening came, he had to sit with her again at the table. It was very strange. One would have thought that nothing had happened on this day or the days before. Her face was as free from shadow as the face of the sky on a clear May day and, as she set out the dishes on the table, she was singing under her breath. He could only wonder at her again and, in his heart, he told himself that she was no more than a child.

There was no need for him to talk. She babbled on happily about anything and everything — to him or to the Gray Shadow. It seemed to make no difference to her. Except that the dog answered her every gesture with his eyes and his wagging tail, but the man sat stolid, with a black face of thought.

Once the dishes were washed, she came to him and stood behind his chair. Her shadow leaned across him and fell upon his knees and the black outline of her head on the floor at his feet.

"Do you like me any better, Ben?" she asked him then.

He put up his hand and patted her fingers on his shoulder, but his heart was breaking, and he could not speak. For the more of beauty and of gentleness he saw in her the more deeply anguish ate into his soul.

Afterward he went into a neighboring bedroom to arrange his sleeping quarters there. He had just thrown a mattress on the springs of the bed when the wild, long wail of a wolf rose from the kitchen. He leaped back through the door and saw Mary huddled in a corner, white-faced. The Gray Shadow stood before the door which opened onto the cellar stairs, whining with eagerness and pawing at the lowest crack.

Ben Flinder threw the door open and instantly breathed the scent of smoke. Something was burning in the cellar of the hotel.

# IX

## "PURSUIT"

Had he been hesitant himself, the Gray Shadow would have showed him the way to duty. The great beast flashed past him and reached the bottom of the flight of steps in an instant, snarling savagely as he went. Flinder heard Mary crying out behind him, imploring him not to run into an unknown danger. The fire was already started. It was too late to attempt to quench it.

Ben left that shrilling voice behind him and, plunging down to the foot of the stairs, he hurried on, carrying his lantern in one hand, his revolver, as usual, in the other. For they who started the flames might have remained to make sure that they took hold on the building securely. And if they were interrupted, would they hesitate to shoot down he who interfered? The very fire they had already started would be the means of removing the vestiges of their second crime.

He had not taken half a dozen steps before he met a thick and rolling mass of smoke that half stifled him. He fought his way through it, and so came into the main hallway which ran through the cellar from front to back. Down this the smoke showed before him in whirling drifts, thin white mists under the lantern light, or milky clouds, all sent scurrying by a strong draft behind them, like a sea fog rushing in across the coast hills as the evening closes on a hot day.

At the end of the hallway he passed into a large and half-finished chamber which was used as a sort of rubbish storeroom. Here the smoke rolled up thick and fast, and there was the sharp, repeated snapping of pine wood as the fire took hold upon it and set the pitch expanding and running. He saw the problem at a glance.

An outer door from this room opening beyond the building for the sake of carting in remnants had been pried open. It hung feebly upon one hinge and through it the incendiaries must have passed. Through it, also, the draft was now pouring which was fanning the fire. The Gray Shadow, as though delighted by the confusion and the yellow flash of the flame through the smoke, leaped here and there, snarling and snapping at the fingers of smoke as they curled down at him. He seemed a demon in the midst of destruction.

Ben Flinder fell to work with a will, frantic at the sight of the fire. He saw that only good fortune had kept the flames from being entirely out of control long before this. There was a quantity of boxes and loose boxwood piled up at one side of the chamber, and this the criminals had ignited. They must have left as soon as the match was touched to the pile, confident that their work was done and that the stuff would go up in flame like tinder. But winter damp had entered the cellar of the hotel and soaked through the wood, so that it burned with surprising slowness. Gradually the fire was eating into the mass and in time would engender enough heat to make the whole break into a roaring flame, but in the meantime its progress was merely inch by inch.

First he propped up the broken door to shut off the draft that was fanning the burning wood. Then he began to pry the loose mass of wood from the wall of the building. The pile was heavy and the work was bitterly difficult, for the heat had become intense, and the lack of air that was choking the fire well-nigh stifled Flinder. He managed to get the pile clear from the wall, however. It lay now in a great pyramid in the center of the chamber. And though by moving it, he had temporarily saved the wall from catching, yet in so doing he had loosened the whole mass, and now the flames began to work up through it more freely. He stumbled into the passage toward the hydrant that connected with the big tank that supplied water to the hotel, and there he encountered a figure moving through the smoke masses. It was Mary, bringing two slopping buckets, half filled with water.

He could only gasp at her: "Good girl!" Then, flinging the water at two yellow heads of the fire, he carried them to the hydrant.

In ten minutes, with Mary working nearly as effectively as himself, the task was ended. The room lay weltering in water, and the thick masses of smoke rolled here and there, seeking vainly for an outlet.

They went back together, half strangled, through the reeking hallway and climbed again to the kitchen. There, panting and rubbing the tears from their reddened eyes, they smiled on one another. There is no bond stronger than good work happily finished by laboring hand in hand.

It was only a moment's respite. The prowling form of the Gray Shadow, roving to and fro restlessly across the kitchen floor and rearing to scratch at the door, told Ben Flinder what he should do. Besides he needed but little prompting. The cowardice of this secret attack made his blood boil. What if they had been asleep and the flames had burst suddenly upward from beneath? They must both have died miserably.

He put on a heavy mackintosh, jammed a hat upon his head, and caught up his rifle. He could see through the window that the storm had fallen off, and the wind, changing to another quarter, had scoured the clouds from the sky and left it bright with moonlight. That was hunting weather for one used to the mountains. On his feet he tied snowshoes. Then he was ready, except that provision must first be made for the girl.

She had watched these preparations with alarm but without a word of comment until the snowshoes were securely on his feet. Then she said quietly: "You goin' to trail them, Ben?"

"I'm out for a walk," he answered obliquely. "There ain't much chance of any danger comin' at you while I'm away. But if danger *should* come, look here!"

He led her into the bedroom and gave her the key to the door.

"That'll keep you pretty safe," he said. "If it don't, here's one thing more. Can you use it?" He offered her a revolver, and she took it, nodding.

"But why not let me go with you, Ben?" she pleaded as he turned away.

"You couldn't keep up with me," he answered. "Besides, there might be business that ain't pretty at the end of this here trail. You understand? But are you afeard, Mary?"

He saw her glance hastily about her, as though the dread of loneliness were already beleaguering her. Then she swallowed hard and shook her head.

"Don't bother about me. Only, Ben . . . if there's three or four of 'em . . . ?"

He did not wait for the caution, but waving his hand at her he passed through the kitchen and out the door with the Gray Shadow before him, held hard on a long leash. For here was a need of better eyes and keener senses than his own, and the Gray Shadow might supply what he lacked. He took the brute to the broken door on the farther side of the Hotel Sprague. First he pushed open the door and made sure that the fire was indeed extinguished. Then, after drawing it into place once more, he let the Gray Shadow drag him forward along the trail.

There was no need of the keen nose or the bright eyes of this night hunter for a time. Across the clearing the tracks went clearly marked, and the heart of Ben Flinder rose in him with a fierce hope as he saw that the incendiaries had ventured out without snowshoes. There had been more than one. Of that he could be equally sure. They had walked carefully in single file, one stepping into the footprints of him who went before, but by the quantity of snow that was trodden down at each impression, he knew there must have been several in the party.

Across the clearing in this fashion they entered the thick of the big pines on the farther side, and here there was need of the Gray Shadow every moment. Where the blue-black shadows drowned the footprints from the eyes of the man, the wolf dog followed them without the slightest effort, straining constantly ahead. Through underbrush it was slow going for Flinder with his snowshoes, but through the more open woods and over the treeless stretches he knew that he must be gaining enormously on the fugitives, the more so as they were probably not hastening along their backtrail. What need had they to hasten when they doubtless planned on destroying pursuit with the flames that consumed the hotel itself?

He caught his first glimpse of them from the top of a little hillock that, as he came out of the wood, stood directly above a little hollow. In that hollow three men were trudging slowly along, almost beneath his very feet.

As he dropped to his knees and jerked his rifle forward, he recognized them all. They were all big, but there were degrees of bigness among them. Yonder fellow with the great bushing red whiskers was the eldest of the Lewis boys, still so-called though the youngest of them was well past thirty. The eldest, a man of forty and the organizer of all their misdeeds, a great burly fellow of a thousand crimes and the reputed strength of a grizzly, was Paul Lewis. Behind him in the single file followed Garry Lewis, the tallest of all the brothers, a lanky, unproportioned champ. The final member of the trio was Martin, who had been star witness at the trial of Ben Flinder for the murder of Dick Lohman ten years before.

His voice was booming through the hollow as he walked along, just as it had boomed through the courtroom with such perfect confidence in his story and such fatal effect upon the minds of the jurors on another day.

"Shut up!" commanded the leader of the party. "Keep your mouth shut, Mart."

"Why shouldn't I sing?" answered Martin, the youngest of the Lewis brothers. "Ain't we to have no fun tonight? You wouldn't let us stay to see the hotel go up in smoke. What's wrong with singin'?"

"The hotel ain't goin' to burn no faster because we stay to watch it. But you singin' . . . how can you tell who might hear you?"

"If you're so damned sure that Flinder is burnin' to a crisp in the hotel, who we got to be afraid of?"

"I never said I was sure of Flinder burnin' in the hotel," said Paul Lewis. "He's had enough bad luck. If it changes, darned if it won't turn ag'in' us. You pipe down and lay off the singin' or. . . ."

Here Martin, turning sullenly to kick the snow away from his boots, caught sight of the kneeling figure and the leveled rifle on the hilltop just above them. His frightened shout was like a signal. The three scattered in as many directions. The rifle, exploding in the hands of Flinder, missed its mark as the wolf dog lurched forward, eager for the pursuit.

# X

## "THE FIGHT"

The straining of the Gray Shadow at the leash brought Flinder to his feet and, swinging down the slope, he took after that member of the gang who had taken the course to the right. If it had not been for the start of the Gray Shadow, he promised himself that he could have bagged the entire three. But since he was robbed of them all, he could at least take the leader. He could at least run down big Paul Lewis.

He ran eagerly, therefore, but the course which Lewis took was one along which the snowshoes of the pursuer gave him small advantage. He of the bushing red whiskers kept along a ridge covered with shrubbery and rough with stones. But even so, by the crackling of the brush ahead of him, Flinder knew that he was gaining steadily.

That noise of flight ceased and, as Flinder came to the edge of a clearing shining cold white under the moon, a rifle rang from the opposite bank of the shrubbery. He pitched back behind a tree with the triumphant yell of Paul Lewis in his ear. Still, though it must have seemed that he had fallen with a bullet through his body, the conqueror had no apparent desire to follow up his victory. Once more the brush began to crackle behind him and Flinder, grown desperate, loosed the Gray Shadow to bring the work to a quick end.

That great beast had hung on the leash slavering with fierce impatience. Now he was off like a dim phantom across the snow and disappeared into the brush beyond. As for Ben Flinder, he had hardly raised to his feet and started after when he heard the hoarse, terrible scream of a man in deadly fear or pain.

He hurried on, the blood congealing in his veins. He broke through the undergrowth and came on a little hollow, nearly naked of trees and packed, waist deep, in snow. In the center was big Paul Lewis, his leather coat ripped from his back and hanging in tatters, to prove what the first snap of the teeth of the wolf had done. His rifle lay with shattered butt nearby where he had struck at his wolfish assailant and broken the stock against the trunk of a tree. Now a revolver was poised in his hand. But he dared not fire, partly because he doubted his ability to strike the shifting mark as the Gray Shadow wove to and fro in the obscure light, keeping up a soft undertone of snarling and circling ever closer for another leap at his quarry. And partly, perhaps, the big man considered that nothing but a mortal wound could keep the beast from leaping at him and tearing his throat out.

"Lewis!" called Flinder.

"Call off this devil and I'll surrender to you, Flinder . . . call him off!"

The last was a yell of fright as the big beast crouched for the spring. Yet a single word from the master brought the Gray Shadow skulking and snarling to his feet.

"Stick up your hands, Lewis," said Flinder, looking down the steady barrel of his rifle. "Stick 'em up high."

Paul Lewis obeyed without a word. Panting heavily, he scanned his antagonist from head to foot, seeming to read something new in him every moment. Standing there with his arms upraised, he himself seemed a towering monster capable of crushing the other into the ground. In fact, he was amazingly without fear.

"I see you've turned thief, Flinder," he said calmly, as the latter extracted two revolvers and a long knife from his captive. "Ain't you got money to buy guns for yourself?"

"Don't start laughin'," warned Flinder. "You ain't goin' to be laughin' so much when you get through with this here!"

"Ain't I?" sneered Lewis. "All right, m'son. You step along and show me why not."

"Why, you fool," said Flinder, and at the anger in his voice the Gray Shadow bristled with a growl, "do you think it'd be anything to me if I dropped you here with a slug through your head?"

"What d'you want out of me?" went on Lewis calmly. "And did you get warmed up before you left the hotel? Dog-gone me if it ain't funny that we can't see the fire from over here." He scanned the sky carelessly. "Maybe the moon's too bright," he added.

"The hotel ain't burnin'," said Flinder quietly.

The other started. "What keeps it back from burnin' then?"

"The wood was pretty damp," said Flinder. "You should have had some oil to give it a start. What a skunk you are, Lewis!"

The latter lowered his arms.

"Keep up your hands!" snapped out Flinder.

"You got my knife and my guns," sneered the other. "Are you still afraid of me?" And he began to brush his thick mustaches, watching Flinder out of ratty little eyes.

"Afraid of you?" said Flinder. He smiled at Lewis without mirth. "Put up them hands," he said again. "I don't aim to bother

65

myself arguin' none with you. If it comes to that, I'd as soon let the gun talk for me."

Lewis shrugged his shoulders. "You ain't a fool," he said without concern. "You ain't goin' to do no murder. You've seen the insides of a prison already. You remember it too damned strong."

The teeth of Flinder showed beneath his curling lip. "I can tell 'em that you tried to burn the hotel."

"You could tell 'em that, but would they believe you? They know that you took this job at the hotel so's you could come gunnin' for us. You wouldn't have a chance."

"Who would find your body?" asked Flinder.

"Murdered men turn up ag'in," said Lewis with profound conviction. "You know that as well as I know it, I guess. Now, what d'you want with me? I'm gettin' cold standin' out here. What you want, old son?"

"I got some paper along with me," said Flinder. "I'll have you write down the name of them that bought the testimony of you gents at the trial ten years back."

"It ain't no use, Flinder. You can't bluff me."

"Suppose I was to put away my own guns. Suppose that I was to start in persuadin' you, Lewis?"

"With your hands?" sneered Lewis. "Are you crazy enough to tackle *me*, Flinder?" And he struck his broad breast with his fist. Truly he was a Hercules. Even Flinder bulked small beside him. But he added: "The wolf would take your side. I wouldn't stand a chance with him."

"I'll fix the wolf," said Flinder, and so saying he tied the Gray Shadow to the trunk of a sapling. Then he turned to the big man again.

"Are you ready, Paul?"

"You got your guns on you."

Flinder jerked the revolver out and tossed it into a bush. A

66

shower of snow fell and left the shrub black in the moonlight. Then Lewis stretched out his great arms.

"Flinder," he said, "ten years ago you used to have sense. It ain't hard to see that you lost it all in prison. Dog-gone me if I ain't pretty near sorry for you." With that, he rushed like a bull.

The Gray Shadow, watching, crouched with his belly in the snow then leaped forward, but the stout rope checked him in mid-air and brought him tumbling to the ground. A great fluff of the dry, powdery snow flew up around him, breaking the force of the fall. He regained his feet again, with green, glaring eyes out of the shadow of the trees. He tugged at the leash. Its strength was too great for him. He turned his head and slashed at it, severing one of the strands as cleanly as though a knife had touched them but, as though there were too much to see, he turned again from that work and watched the scene in the hollow.

Then he strained eagerly forward, his great red mouth open and the shining fangs prepared, but there came into his reach only a shower of snow dust. He snarled with furious disappointment and lay down on his belly again, growling, shuddering with his rage. He could understand this thing; it was the same brute story which all beasts of prey know by heart.

Now he stood erect again, his hair bristling, his head dropped, a shudder passing through his strong body. After that, he backed up slowly until his rump touched the trunk of the tree behind him at which he leaped forward with a startled yelp very like the frightened cry of any house dog. But all the while his eyes never left the scene that was enacted before him.

At last his tail began to wag. He whined suddenly and, lifting his head, some of the green went out of his eyes. The great form of Ben Flinder staggered back to him. One trailing hand touched the head of the big wolf dog.

What a change was this in Flinder? His clothes were a torn wreck. The snowshoes on his feet were reduced to a wrecked tangle. He was powdered white with snow from head to foot, and steam rose from him, turning the snow rapidly into little trickles of water. A tremor ran through his body constantly. Yet his head was high.

"Get up!" he gasped out.

A groan answered him. Paul Lewis heaved himself up on shuddering arms that collapsed and let him fall back again in the snow.

Flinder went and stood over him. He took the big man by the red hair of his head and wrenched him brutally into a sitting posture. "Have you got enough?" he asked.

"I got enough," groaned Lewis.

He sat with his head hanging upon his breast and his arms trailing limply at his side.

"Can you hold a pencil?" asked Flinder.

"I dunno."

"Try it then."

He drew out a long envelope and a pencil. "Here's my pardon," he said. "And here's a pencil. Now, Lewis, I want the truth, understand?"

"About what, Ben?"

"Who brought you up . . . you and the rest of your gang . . . to talk ag'in' me at the trial?"

"It was Sprague."

"Hell and fire! D'you aim to want to make me believe that?"

"It was Sprague, I tell you."

"You lie!"

Before the threatening form of Flinder, the beaten man cringed with something like a sob of weak helplessness.

"I ain't able to think of no lies, Flinder. I got to tell you the truth."

68

"Why should Sprague . . . it ain't possible?"

"He hated Dick Lohman. I found that out afterward. He wanted to get rid of him. He hired Lefty Ginnis to do the trick, and he hired us to accuse you and talk ag'in' you. Is that clear?"

"Why should he hate Lohman?"

"I dunno. Something about Sprague's niece. I dunno what."

"Who'd've thought that?" said Flinder. He added: "And what set you to tryin' to burn the hotel?"

"Sprague wouldn't come through with all the money that he'd promised us for talkin' at the trial. He give us a first payment. After that he put us off with promises until last summer. Then he said that if we talked ag'in' him, we wouldn't be believed, and anyways, what we said would be as bad for ourselves as for him. Understand? So we aimed to get even with the old liar."

"So you came at the hotel this winter?"

"Just now? Nope, it was Sprague that set us at the hotel just now."

"Sprague ag'in! Am I crazy, maybe? D'you think I'm a fool, Lewis?"

"It sounds queer. But Sprague got his insurance on the hotel, and then he aimed to have it burned. It wasn't payin' him much up here of a summer. It was losin' money for him, maybe. Anyway, he come to us a few days ago and give us all the back money he'd promised and added a lot more if we'd burn the hotel. That's all that I know."

"It's enough," said Flinder. "Write it down!"

# XI

## "MARY DISAPPEARS"

He came back toward the Sprague Hotel slowly. There was no leash on the Gray Shadow, but that great animal walked at the heel of his new-found master as though held in place there by collar and chain. Who can say that there is not an electric wire running from mind to mind, even from man to beast? There had not been a word spoken, and yet the Gray Shadow stole along behind the big man as though a whip were hanging over his head.

Ben Flinder, walking through the pale, cold moonlight, with the confession of Paul Lewis in his pocket, felt that the world was his. It was his fondest dream come true. The law that had stolen ten years from him and given him ten eternities of pain instead, had now been placed at his service. That which had struck him down must now strike down his enemies.

When he thought of all the implications of that confession of Lewis's, he could have laughed aloud with his joy. It meant swift and complete ruin for the Lewis boys and their outlawry, if they refused to submit to arrest. It meant, perhaps, the hanging of Thomas Sprague, that shrewd old rat of a financier. And while this summary justice was being poured forth upon the heads of those who had long deserved it, Ben Flinder might sit by without so much as lifting his hand and enjoy the suffering of those who fell under the hand of the law.

He began to consider that long-hated abstraction from a new position. It had been the whip that lashed him. Now the butt of the whip was in his hand, and the lash would fall upon others. That hand of the law that had struck him down could strike down seven or seven hundred fully as easily as it had managed him. He looked back upon his career in the penitentiary, upon the faces of the men in the jury box, upon the wild harangue of Charles Sumner, eager to make his fame as a prosecutor secure. He considered the solemn, sad face of the judge, weighing and sifting evidence, with labor shadowing his eyes like grief. He remembered the curious eyes that had fixed upon him from the instant that he was arrested for the murder of Dick Lohman. He remembered the hard-handed, sharp-voiced guards in the penitentiary. How he had hated them! How he had sought to rebel against them. With what cruel scorn and pleasure they had crushed him with their power. The solitary stretches of confinement — the hardest and filthiest labor that could be found for him — and then the maddening horror of the dark cell.

He had gone mad with hatred of society and society's laws in those years. He still shuddered as he recalled them. But now he was beginning to understand a little more clearly that which had happened to him. He could conceive of the law as a monster eager to protect a great flock of helpless sheep. Now and then the wolves ran in from the shadows and stole a sheep away, and the monster hand of the giant, sweeping blindly down, might crush another sheep, thinking that it had found the wolf. So it was with the law. There was no malice. But like all human things the law could be mistaken and, when it was mistaken, its cruelty had a doubly-edged tooth.

These were the things that Ben Flinder turned in his brain as he went back through the snow toward the Sprague Hotel. Half way along the trail the moon suddenly went out. He looked up and saw thick masses of clouds, hanging so wonderfully low that they covered the head and half the sides of huge Mount Comas, sweeping up from the south. A full half of the sky was already blotted out. And still the changing wind rolled the clouds farther and farther north and, now, in ranks of black, broken with fugitive glimpses of fleecy white where the moon broke

71

dimly through here and there, the clouds pushed against the southern faces of Druid and Erskine and Hastings mountains that filled the hollow to the north. A moment more and the whole northern horizon was black, and the earth, at the same time, grew black likewise. The trees were masses of deepest shadow, and even the white face of the snowy, open stretches was dulled. The big horizon which had swept around him on every side was blotted out. For a moment or two he made out misshapen, rudely sketched outlines of the northern mountains; then these dissolved in thicker blackness. He had not gone on for five minutes more when a sharp wind began to cut at his face, stooping down into the deep bosom of the hollow, and a little later he was wrapped in a driving fog.

No sea fog ever moved as this was doing. Instead of streaming across from Mount Comas toward Erskine and Justice mountains, through some freak of the currents of the upper air the clouds were forced down like a waterfall crashing down from a height. Those clouds were ice cold, dense masses of vapor, driven at the speed of express trains making up time. Ben Flinder had to give his shoulder to them and lean against them at a sharp slant. As for his way, he lost all track of it after the second time he stumbled and fell upon his knees. When he put a leash on the Gray Shadow, the wolf dog led him straight forward. Perhaps it was toward the hotel — perhaps it was toward some forest haunt of the great brute's. Ben Flinder could not tell until the leash suddenly grew slack and then, peering before him, he made out the dim outlines of Sprague Hotel. He went forward and blundered up a short flight of steps. In fact, the unerring instinct of the wolf dog had taken him in a straight line through the whirling cloud masses to the kitchen door of the hotel.

Ben observed with a smile that Mary had obeyed his orders so strictly that she had not even yet ventured out from the bedroom to build a fire in the kitchen and light the lamps there.

72

The window was a black rectangle with a wet face from the sweep of the clouds. He thrust the door open and called cheerfully: "Hello! Mary! It's Ben come back ag'in!"

He waited, smiling. The smile went out, for not a whisper answered him. He cried in anger: "It ain't a time for playin' no game, Mary. Holler out and let me hear your voice!"

Waiting again for an answer, he heard a long, thin echo take up his voice and repeat it. It must mean, therefore, that the door to the outer hall was open, and that was odd. He distinctly remembered that the door had been locked when he left the building earlier in the night. Certainly it was odd that Mary should have opened it of her own free will.

Here a cold thought struck upward to his brain and made him half sick. He fumbled hastily for the lantern, found it on its peg, and lighted it, turning in time to see the Gray Shadow disappear through the open doorway from the kitchen leading into the long main corridor of the first floor of the hotel. The wolf dog passed out from the kitchen through a curling wraith of fog that had blown thickly through the outside door of the kitchen and was now filling the room like moth wings or numberless flying ghosts.

He gave his first glance to the disappearing figure of the Gray Shadow. He gave his second toward the door of the bedroom, and there he saw the tragedy written clearly for him and with a single word, so to speak. For the bedroom door was split and shattered down the middle. One half lay upon the floor. The other sagged open upon the hinges.

He stumbled blindly into the next room. As he went, he saw there were three or four round, neatly drilled holes in the hanging part of the door. He had no need to measure them. That measure he carried about with him in his mind; the holes had been drilled by forty-five caliber bullets.

That her assailants could have fired in upon her was incredible.

No, she had stood at bay while they threatened her and commanded her to open the door to them. At last, infuriated by the delay, they had caught up something — ay, yonder it was — a stoutly built chair, reduced to a splintered wreck. With that as a club they had begun to batter down the door until Mary emptied her revolver through it in a vain endeavor to keep them away. The door had gone down and, before she could reload, they were rushing into the room. Even so she had not submitted. She must have been filled with a blind terror — a nightmare thing. See where she had clutched at the bed, as if that inanimate thing might protect her! They had torn her ruthlessly away. The bedclothes were scattered on the floor; the mattress was awry. They had torn her away and carried her back through the kitchen — yonder was the scrape of a spur along the floor — and so out into the night.

He himself reached again the outer door of the kitchen, and there he paused. The rolling fog billowed like milk-white smoke against his face. He could not see a hand's breadth before him. What should he do then, attempt to trail the girl and those who had assailed her?

In a stupor he sat down, holding in his hands a glove that lay on the kitchen floor. All at once it seemed to Ben Flinder no larger than the glove of a child, and tears of pity stung his eyes. He started up, panting, for he felt that his breath was leaving him. It was a marvelously empty room. The big stove on the one side was sweating with the congealed moisture. Wherever he looked through the thick-flocking drifts of the entering fog, he made out hints and glimmerings of a form.

He felt, at that, he would go mad if he remained there long. While he stared helplessly about him, he saw the Gray Shadow come back into the room, his head low, scenting on a trail. He reached the master and gave his nose with studious care to the glove which Ben Flinder was holding. The Gray

Shadow whined in recognition.

He dropped his head again and made for the outer door. There he paused, then looking back with a whine to Ben Flinder, he disappeared into the outer night.

It did not take Flinder long to follow. For here was a hint which did not need to be expressed in words but which said more plainly: *"Follow me! Follow me! I can find her if you will follow."*

Flinder was out through the door in an instant, his rifle in his hand, running through the dark and calling aloud. Before him he heard the whine of the wolf dog. That was his guiding light. He drove after it through the murky night. He fixed the leash on the Gray Shadow again, and once more, blindly, he let the great brute lead him.

They headed straight south. They were climbing the slope of Mount Comas. So much he knew, but what part of the slope they were on he could not tell. He only knew that the Gray Shadow never slackened the pace, never ceased to lean forward mightily against the leash and help along the struggling man behind him. Thinking how fearfully he depended now upon the great dog, he swore on the spot that all dumb beasts should from that instant be dear to him.

They drew up higher on the mountain. Presently they passed into a region where the fog began to turn from dingy deep gray to shining white. The fog grew thinner. Glimpses of the stars appeared. Then, suddenly, the fog disappeared like a wave and left him in the moonlight again. They had actually climbed above the clouds.

Yet they were still on the very dividing line. He was buried to the knees in the solid white smoke of the clouds. The Gray Shadow showed only head and shoulders and tip of the tail above that mysterious bath. Then the wave heaved up and they were swallowed again — a dizzy thing after having been for an instant in a clear light.

But the Gray Shadow was not confused. He kept on at the same gait. Still they climbed, and now the fog definitely receded. They were on a broad shoulder of Mount Comas, a wide, thick western shoulder, wading through the snow in thick drifts, or planting wet feet upon dangerously smooth rocks from which the storm had polished away the whirling snow.

Never had Ben Flinder seen a sight more magnificent. All around him was the moon-shining beauty of the heavens with a fresh, crisp south wind blowing into his face, but not a wind of any bitter coldness. It seemed, indeed, almost warm to Ben Flinder at moments as he walked along.

Beneath him the white ocean of the clouds rushed northward, pushing in waves big as mountains that tossed up gigantic heads one instant and then were torn to pieces by the wind that made them the next. The thick white billows washed over the mountain forest and blotted it from sight. It seemed to Flinder, looking west, that he stood on a solitary pinnacle of rock — all that was left of the round earth's nations, for all the rest had been overwhelmed in this strange sea of vapor, hurtling ever from the south pole toward the north with a dizzy speed that made his eyes reel as it rushed beneath his feet. In his ears there was music fit for the ending of the world, the shrill screaming of the wind sometimes in single voices and sometimes deep and far-off choruses of the storm. He was half delighted, half appalled, and almost relieved when the Gray Shadow led him on beneath the blanket of the mist.

# XII

## "AT KINKAID'S RANCH"

They swung twice on the left, coming down on the farther side
of the big mountain, and in the end, far beneath the cloud level
with the night thick before his face and the snow deep underfoot,
he was brought before a long, low-lying house with the bulky
outlines of great barns looming vaguely through the dark in a
half circle behind the farm house. This must be the residence
of some rich and powerful rancher, and the heart of Ben Flinder
sank a little.

For money, he knew, was a great enemy. It could raise a hundred hands against him, lay on his head a reward that would
bring out every able-bodied man in the mountains and desert,
and shrink the walls together until he was run down and de-
stroyed. He thought of these things as he scowled toward the
long roof of the building and the many yellow squares of light
that broke through its black sides. Then he came nearer. To
have the Gray Shadow with him was to be possessed of a walking
danger that might betray him at any instant with a snarl. So
he tied the leash of the great wolf dog to a fence post not far
from the house and went on with his explorations.

He came past a square building from which a jangle of voices
issued, rough, loud voices interrupting one another without ceremony, a familiar sound to Flinder. By the number of voices
he could judge the size of the ranch, and he decided that it must
be a huge one. At least, by the uproar in the bunkhouse, Ben
Flinder decided that there must be from twelve to twenty men
housed there. He flattened himself near the door and listened.

It was hard to decipher any main thread of conversation. There
was a general babel. Half a dozen voices were always sounding

at once. He paused there for a whole ten minutes, with his limbs growing stiff with the cold and his ears turning so crisp that he felt as though they would break off like frozen leaves at the first touch. But finally he had a reward: "When I asked the old man where she'd been, he'd allowed she'd been off payin' a visit to. . . ."

"D'you believe that?"

"The devil, man, I ain't no fool. And I ain't a big enough fool to let the old man think that I don't believe what he tells me. What he says is plenty good enough for me. He's dangerous, that old devil. That's what he is."

"Are you talkin' about Mary?" broke in another voice and, at that, as though a word of magic had been pronounced, a silence fell suddenly across the bunkhouse.

"We're talkin' about Mary."

"Then tune up on something else, partners. There ain't no use hopin' for her. He's got her back now, and it'll be a cold day before she gets away ag'in."

"She's just been off visitin', the old man says."

There was a rumble from the others.

"She won't do no visitin' no more. He's got Josh McCormick and Bud Rivers watchin' her. I aim to say that Josh and Bud'll take care she don't go gaddin' no more."

"What did she plan on?"

"Just gettin' shut of the old devil. So long, boys. I gotta see that fool mare ain't frettin' herself to death."

With this the door swung open, a shaft of dull lantern light struck out into the night, and a big man jumped down to the ground. His next step, before Flinder could move, carried his foot against the ribs of the eavesdropper and sent the cowpuncher sprawling as the door slammed to behind him. Before he could make an outcry, Flinder had him by the throat.

"You feel this under your chin, old son? It ain't a chunk of ice. It's the nose of a Colt. But it ain't goin' to bark at you if you do what you're told to do. Understand? Now, stand up."

He released his hold, and the man rose with him to his feet.

"Now," said Flinder, when he had led his captive around to the side of the bunkhouse, "tell me where Mary's room is in the house."

The cowpuncher started. "It ain't no good," he declared. "She's bein' watched. . . ."

"Look here," said Flinder. "I know all about that. But I want to know where her room is."

"What good'll that be to you?"

"That ain't the question."

"What good'll it be to *her?*" said the 'puncher.

"I ain't got time to explain."

"Then I'll talk no more."

It amazed Flinder and delighted him, this quiet courage and defiance.

"Partner," he said. "I aim to say that you're somethin' of a man. I'll tell you this much. I'm the party that she's been visitin'."

"You are? What was in her head?"

"I figure marriage is in our heads, friend."

"The devil!"

"I'm tellin' you straight." He had risked that statement blindly. If the girl were already married, he would at least be able to learn the fact.

"But you know . . . ," began the cowpuncher. "Why, the old man'll go crazy," he added. "Him having brought a husband for her all the way from New York!"

"But," said Flinder, hoping against hope, "she ain't married the New Yorker yet."

"She ain't. But they've sent for the minister. D'you know that?"

"She can't be forced if she. . . ."

"Forced? Her uncle'll force an angel to do what he wants,

if he gets a chance. Didn't he make her get engaged to this gent before she ever clapped eyes on the skinny little runt?"

"Maybe so," said Flinder, a light of joy breaking in upon his mind. "But all I'm askin' of you is . . . where's her room?"

"I see you're dead set on makin' a corpse out of yourself."

"Maybe so."

"Then . . . by heaven, I like the way you talk. If she's for you, I'm for you. You talk our lingo anyway. Look there. The third window from the end of the house. That's her room. I guess maybe she's in it now."

"Thanks," said Ben Flinder. "Now, old son, what'm I goin' to do with you? Do I have to tie you up and leave you out here in the snow to freeze to death for fear of you lettin' out a yap and givin' me away?"

"You play your own hand," said the cowpuncher calmly. "But I dunno that I'd let out no yap. I'm lookin' to go out to the barn and see how a mare of mine is gettin' on that I just bought yesterday in Comas."

That town's name made Ben Flinder start but, remembering the torturous way in which the trail after the girl had carried him through the mountains, he was not greatly surprised to find that they had circled back into the vicinity of the town.

"Suppose that we shake hands on it?" said Ben Flinder.

"Here's my hand, partner."

They shook hands in the dark.

"I wish you luck," added the 'puncher, "but I tell you that they's two big-sized gents mighty handy with their guns standin' watch under her window. Or else that's where they're supposed to be until the minister comes and splices the girl to the gent from New York. You'll have to take a long chance, old son."

"Thanks," said Flinder. "That sort of long chance is just in my line. Understand?"

"Might I know your name?"

"You'll be hearin' that name before tomorrow night, most like. So long, partner."

"So long, chief."

So they parted, and neither, from that instant, ever laid eyes on the other again.

# XIII

## "SETTLED WITHOUT LEGAL WARFARE"

The wealth of Kinkaid had been founded in a time when men were more plentiful than money in the West. Out of those hard old days he retained many customs, and one of them was to keep saddled, day and night, four fast horses. Those four saddles were filled swiftly now with his own redoubtable self and three of his best fighting men on a ranch where all were warriors of some repute. Once in the saddle they rode toward the town of Comas. For when old Kinkaid had sent for Mary, her escape from her room through the window had been discovered. Kinkaid had rushed outside. A dozen lanterns had been brought at once, and there lay the trail in the snow, clear as though printed with ink across white paper. In the snow at the side of the building he had come on the form of Josh McCormack, lying tied and gagged, and this same fate had befallen Bud Rivers, his second guard.

Now Kinkaid himself, with a lantern, led the way, and it was he who read the sign of the trail. After the start he could do it at a canter, and so they swept briskly forward. The trail left the road at once and passed across the fields until it struck in toward the town just behind the house of the minister, young Edgar Athelstane.

The elation of Kinkaid passed all bounds. "We've run 'em right down to the ground," he said. "If the fools had hid out, they might've got away, but takin' to the earth like this . . . damn my eyes, I think they must've gone to the minister's house."

They rounded to the front of that dwelling, hard beside the church with its narrow, sky-pricking steeple. There, with his three men shoulder to shoulder behind him, the rancher advanced to the front door of the house. He had warned his 'punchers beforehand.

"Unless I miss my guess, partners, this lad that stole Mary is a hell-bent fightin' fool. Keep your guns ready."

Then he knocked at the door.

It was close to morning, but the minister himself opened the door. He was seen dressed and huddled into a bathrobe for the sake of warmth.

"You're Athelstane, the minister," said Kinkaid.

"You're Kinkaid, the rancher," said the minister.

"That's me. You got my niece here in your house, Athelstane?"

The reply came smoothly enough: "I have."

"Thank heaven! Well, young man, you don't have to bother no more with her. You can turn her right over to me."

"That," said Athelstane, "I am not prepared to do."

Kinkaid recoiled a step. "By the heavens, Athelstane," he cried, "if I got to use force, I'll use it. Are you helpin' out at a kidnappin'?"

"How old is your niece?" asked Athelstane.

"No more'n eighteen her last birthday, and. . . ."

"She's of age, man. In this state a woman has the right to marry, without the consent of a guardian, at the age of eighteen. What right have you over her?"

"Right?" thundered the rancher. "All the right in the world! Who *has* a better right over her?"

"No one, my friend, until she takes a husband."

82

Kinkaid made a sign, and all four shouldered forward. Athelstane exposed a hand which bore a revolver.

"If I fire this weapon into the floor," he said, "the noise will bring twenty men around us in as many seconds. You will then have to answer for breaking into the home of a law-abiding citizen without a warrant. In that case I think every one of you will be liable to a prison sentence and, by heaven, Mister Kinkaid, I'll see that you get it!"

The rancher was a man of passion. He was a man of sense, also. He was able to judge a man in half a dozen seconds. He read the big minister now, and he read him aright.

"Athelstane," he said, "lemme in to talk to that fool girl."

"Certainly," said the minister and, admitting the big man, he stepped back and locked the door in the faces of the three cowpunchers.

As for Kinkaid he walked with his rolling gait of an old horseman into the living room of the cottage. There he found that Mary Kinkaid had risen to greet him and at her side a big man with a strangely white face — a pallor familiar to those who have been through the cells of a prison. It needed only one glance. Then Kinkaid slumped into a chair.

"It's Ben Flinder!" he exclaimed. "I might've knowed that. It's Flinder."

"It's me," said Flinder gently.

"You fool," cried Kinkaid to his niece. "Are you aimin' to marry a no-account jailbird?"

At his voice Mary winced and lost color. But instead of answering him directly, she shrank against the side of her companion and looked up to his face with a half frightened smile.

"I dunno that there's much sense to it," said Ben Flinder. "But she thinks that she sees somethin' in me that might be made into the sort of a man that could take care of her. Leastwise, she knows that I don't aim to sell her, Kinkaid."

83

* * * * *

It was the expectation of the entire town that a mighty legal war would be raised by the great Kinkaid, but they were strangely disappointed. As he himself said publicly: "I know when I'm licked. I'm gettin' old, maybe. Anyway, Flinder beat me."

Before the week was out, Mr. and Mrs. Ben Flinder removed to the Kinkaid ranch. Old Kinkaid himself went south. He had been wanting a vacation, he declared, for years, but he had never been able to find a real man to leave in charge of the ranch until now.

"A prison eddication," said Kinkaid, "is what most of these here 'punchers need to round 'em out."

After that the affairs of Ben Flinder were somewhat forgotten in Comas. They were covered over by the excitement attending the trial and the sentencing of old Thomas Sprague and by the pursuit of the Lewis boys. But the latter had fled and scattered over the country. Not one of them was ever brought to justice.

As for the hotel, it is still standing. Its only known occupant is a gray wolf.

Street & Smith's *Western Story Magazine*, the foremost Western pulp magazine especially from the time when Frederick Faust began contributing to it regularly in late 1920, fell on hard times in 1932 because of the effects on sales of the Depression and competition from other magazine publishers, above all Popular Publications with *Dime Western* and, in 1933, *Star Western*. Frank E. Blackwell, editor of *Western Story Magazine*, wanted to cut Faust's word rate from 5¢ to 4¢ a word and finally succeeded in doing so but at a price. For the year 1934 Faust's agent pre-sold 200,000 words to Popular Publications, most of these short novels appearing in *Star Western* under the Max Brand byline and helping to establish this magazine as a staple with the reading public. The story that follows was the fourth short novel by Max Brand to be showcased in *Star Western*. It appeared in the July, 1934 issue.

# GALLOWS GAMBLE

# I

## "WET CATTLE AND HOT MONEY"

Jack Sherry was so big that he could not trust one mustang to carry him through a day's journey. Therefore some people called him "Two-Horse" Jack. He was so big that he could look eye to eye with that border giant and dealer in wet cattle, Jumbo Joe. A few declared that he was as strong as Jumbo. Yet this was not generally believed, for such strength as Jumbo Joe's is terrible, and it was hard to fear handsome, careless, smiling Jack Sherry.

As he rode now, he held his head back a little and sent a song thundering over the backs of the Mexican cattle. They were accustomed to that voice by this time. It had given the cattle assurance during night storms and had herded them through the day. Now the familiar sound took some of the wildness out of their eyes. The Rio Grande was not far away, and this was the last trip he needed to make with wet cattle.

He looked over these steers with a peculiar satisfaction. They were bony in the hips, gaunted in the belly, but good Texas grazing land would soon fill out their Mexican hides with solid meat. They had been bought cheap, and they would sell quite high if Jumbo Joe stuck to the price upon which he had agreed. Carefully driven from water to water across the northern desert of Mexico, they were finishing the journey in good condition.

A sharp, yipping cry came from the other side of the herd, and Jack Sherry grinned when he marked the voice. He always smiled when he heard Bill Garvin sing out like a yelping coyote. Garvin was ten years his senior, but friendship had welded them together more closely than fire and hammers ever welded steel. A lean, sun-dried man, Bill Garvin came up with his mustang at a lope. He swung in beside Sherry.

"Something coming from the west," he said. "Look!"

Sherry stared until he saw the misty rising of dust against the horizon. "You've got eyes of an Indian, Bill," he said. "What is it? Cattle?"

"Riders," said Garvin. "Get the wool out of your brain and notice how fast that dust is growing. Cattle never traveled that fast. Besides, there ain't enough dust for a cattle drive."

"You're right," agreed Sherry. "Riders . . . Mexicans probably. That may mean hell popping."

"Not likely, if we start popping first."

They looked to their saddle-booted Winchesters and, briefly, at one another.

"This being the last trip," said Sherry, "we're apt to tie onto trouble before the finish. Everything's been going too smooth."

The dust cloud dwindled and lifted, and two riders came out from beneath it.

"A boy and a grown man," said Bill Garvin. "We can quit worrying." He added a moment later: "A man and a woman." Then, in surprise: "White!"

"How do you tell that?" asked Sherry.

"I dunno. I don't tell it. I just feel it."

"I'll never get the hang of things the way you have it," sighed Sherry.

"Because there ain't enough meanness in you," answered Garvin. "You never been mad enough to really untie your hands. You never been poisoned enough to wake you up. But one of these days you're gonna come to yourself and then a real Bitter Creek lobo will seem like a sleeping milch cow alongside of you."

88

Sherry shrugged his big shoulders. He was watching the two riders who came on at a steady lope, changing their direction to join the herders.

"It's Tom Carey," said Garvin. "Dog-gone me, I'd rather see the devil than Tom and his questions right now. Sherry, you wake up your jaw and do the answering. There's Paula along with her father. Why don't they stay home and go hunting?"

"What in thunder are they down here for?" wondered Sherry.

It was not until this moment that he was finally able to recognize the two riders who pushed straight ahead. There was a waving of hats and hands and a cordial greeting. Paula Carey began to laugh.

"Where did you pick up this herd?" she asked.

"Just a gift from an old Mexican friend," said Sherry.

"It's no laughing matter," broke in Tom Carey. He had the grim, hard face of a man who had fought his way through life. He had won the fight so far, as his big ranch and his thousands of fat cattle attested. "People are beginning to hear whispers about you two," he went on. "Are these going to be wet cattle?"

"They look pretty dry now," offered Garvin.

"Mind you," said Carey, "I blame you fellows less than I'd blame most. You made your honest start. Bad luck and a crooked banker wiped you out. You're trying to make a new start even if you had to begin outside the law. But I want to tell you that this is a damned bad business. Damned bad! These critters are raised down here at a lot less cost a head than we can raise 'em for over the Rio. You get 'em dirt cheap, drive 'em across the river, and fatten 'em on American grass. Then they invade our market and cheapen prices for the rest of us who raise our cows legitimately and pay decent wages to white men. This has got to be stopped and, by God, it's going to be!" He smacked his fist into his other hand and glowered. "Where did you get these steers?" he demanded.

"We bought 'em from an old one-legged widow woman, Mister Carey," said Jack Sherry. "She has five children and not a drop of tequila in the house. It's charity to help widows and orphans."

Carey frowned, shaking his head, but Jack Sherry could see his anger dissolving into a smile.

"How old are the five children, Jack?" asked the girl.

"From twenty up," said Sherry. "The hungriest lot of Mexicans I ever saw. They bit every coin we paid 'em."

"Come along, Paula," said her father. "We've got to forget that we've seen a pair of smugglers."

"These cattle aren't wet yet," said the girl. "How long are you two sticking with this business?"

"The last trip," answered Sherry. "Am I coming to see you?"

"You're taking me to the dance on Saturday," she told him.

"He's a cattle smuggler . . . and you're going to dance with him?" growled Carey.

"There's so much of him that he can't be good all over," said the girl. "So long, boys. I'll be seeing you."

She started away beside her father, their fine horses stretching out into a swinging lope.

Bill Garvin shook his head as he looked after them. "There's a pair of real clean-bred ones," he said.

"You mean the horses, eh?" asked Sherry, grinning.

"I mean the riders. Where did you get the idea of talking about widows and orphans?"

"It's the truth, isn't it?" asked Sherry.

"I wish they'd seen those orphans getting pie-eyed," sighed Garvin. "I wish they'd seen you knock their heads together when they started the knife-pulling. And I wish they knew the kind of a nacheral-born and educated liar you are, Jack."

"They know," answered Sherry.

"They know there ain't any meanness in you," said Garvin. "Which I wish there was more. Meat has to be salted, or it's

90

likely to spoil. What d'you do to the girls, Jack?"

"What do you mean?"

"I mean, how do you fish their hearts up into their throats and make their eyes shine like a cow with a knock-kneed calf beside it?"

"You're wrong," argued Sherry. "She's just a friend. There's no nonsense about Paula."

"No, there's no nonsense about her," growled Garvin. "There's nothing but marriage and children and a lot of damn' serious stuff like that when she looks at you. Hey! Get that fool misery-brindled steer back into the herd!"

It was late evening when they reached the Rio Grande. Bill Garvin, coming up to point, eased some of the herd down the bank and into the wide shallows of the river, while Sherry industriously applied pressure on the rear. Presently the entire living mass was drinking, wading, rolling through the dull currents towards the American shore.

When the last gaunted steer was up the bank, Garvin held the leading stragglers while Sherry, from the rear, pushed the cattle into a compact mass. The last sunset color had ended when a pair of riders came out of the brush.

"Haloo-oo!" called a great voice.

"Jumbo!" shouted Garvin in answer.

All four riders gathered together. Even by starlight the immense, distorted face of Jumbo Joe was visible enough. Tex Walton, his lieutenant, seemed to be lost in the shadows of the night. But left to himself, Tex was well worth consideration, particularly in a gunfight. Eight notches had been filed into each bone grip of his two .45s — and it was said that those sixteen dead men represented only a little more than half the total of his victims. Every man in the southwest part of the state knew that Walton and Jumbo Joe lived by crime, but not a soul had been able to put either of them behind the bars.

"We got the full number and twenty over," said Bill Garvin. "All in the right condition on the trail, too. We didn't burn 'em up making the last stages."

"I seen they was the right number," said Jumbo in his peculiar, snarling voice. "I seen they was the right condition, too, by the way they hopped up the bank. And here's your seven thousand."

"Count out the money," said Sherry.

"My word ain't good enough for you, eh?" demanded Jumbo truculently.

"Mister," said Sherry good naturedly, "the best sort of men make mistakes . . . and you're not the best sort."

For a fraction of a second Jumbo stiffened. The others were suddenly tense and silent, sensing the imminence of battle. Then Jumbo relaxed. "I'm lettin' that one ride for a while," he said in his great, hoarse voice. "You're only a kid, Sherry, but you wanta mind who you're talking to. *Sabe?*"

"Thanks," said Sherry. "I'm glad to take advice from a gent who knows what he's talking about. Hold a light, Bill, while I count this stuff."

The money was secured inside a band of brown paper that held the bills in a stiff sheaf. Bill Garvin held a match in the cup of his hands. Sherry counted the bills quickly, flicking the corners where the denominations were printed.

"Just one thousand shy," he announced finally.

"You lie!" said Jumbo. "You palmed some of it if it ain't all there."

"Watch Tex," said Sherry to his partner. "I'll take care of the big fellow . . . ! All right, Jumbo, so I'm a liar, am I? And what else have you got to say?"

"A ornery . . . ," commenced Jumbo Joe, thundering.

"Wait a minute. Is this business, or ain't it?" asked Tex.

"Here's the money back, and we'll keep the steers," said Sherry.

"Times are rotten," complained Jumbo. "You don't know how rotten they are! Six thousand bucks is a hell of a lot of hard cash, and here it is. No waiting. You get the cash payment on the nail!"

"Seven thousand . . . and you're getting some extra head of steers at that," insisted Sherry.

"Here. Give him another thousand," said Jumbo Joe.

"It's a fool trick to bluff like that," remarked Tex Walton.

"Maybe. But I've saved a lot of *dinero* that same way."

Walton passed across ten hundred bills more.

"All right, Tex," said Jumbo Joe. "Swarm in and move those steers. So long, Garvin. Sherry, I'll be remembering you."

Towards Travis Junction, towards a new beginning in life, with seven thousand dollars in the pocket of the younger partner, rode Sherry and Bill Garvin.

"It's all ours, and it's all clear," said Sherry. "It's all dirty money, Bill, but we'll make it right with some years of good clean work. We know the land we want on lease, and we know where we can buy cheap cattle to stock it. What could be better?"

"We need one dead man planted before we're in the clear," answered Bill Garvin, who was a thoughtful man. "Jumbo will never leave your trail until he's tangled with you once more. Nobody else ever made him back up the way you did tonight. He won't be forgetting."

"We'll play with Jumbo when he starts a deal," said Jack Sherry. "Look at those lights, Bill. Don't they start a thirst in the back of your throat?"

The lights of Travis Junction spread before them like an entangled constellation that had fallen to the earth. Those lights grew until, at a gallop, the partners entered the little town. They were not for a real tear. They had too much money in their hands to be careless in their drinking, but they wanted to have about them, for a moment, the saloon odors, the saloon atmosphere of "tomorrow," and the burn of hard bar whiskey in the back of the throat.

That was why they wound up in Teddy Mallon's Saloon with desert dust sweat caked in their shirts and the starved desert look in their faces. Only three or four other men were in the bar as the pair ranged in front of it, but they gave to Jack Sherry the smile and the friendly greeting that his open, big-featured face always won. He looked up as he poised his glass and smiled at Bill.

"Here's to every day that's coming to us," said Sherry.

"Here's to you, Jack," smiled Garvin.

Down went the drinks. Sherry's hand was still thrown back when he saw a reflective notice floating in the big mirror before him.

### Five Thousand Dollars Reward

"Hello!" said Sherry. "Who done enough to get a five thousand dollar reward posted?" He observed that Ted Mallon, tending bar, was staring wonderingly down at the ten-dollar bill Sherry had given him. "What's the matter, Ted?" he asked. "Never seen that much money all in one heap?"

Mallon, instead of answering, pushed the change across the counter with an almost reluctant hand and went from the bar-room, frowning. Sherry had turned around and was reading the posted notice offering five thousand dollars for the two men who held up the Overland.

"Where you been, Sherry?" asked one of the men in the saloon. "You ain't heard of the train hold-up in During Gulch? They stuck up the Overland, all right. A pair of *hombres,* and one of 'em as big as Jumbo Joe . . . or you!" He laughed, adding: "A gent behind a gun always looks pretty big. They blew open the safe in the mail car and got fifty-sixty thousand bucks. On the way to getting that, they shot a man dead."

"That's too much to pay for sixty thousand," nodded Sherry. "Murder's too much to pay for any money. Hey, where's Ted? We want another drink. Hey, Ted!"

Ted appeared as though in answer to the call, but he came through the swinging front door with three men ahead of him, and one of them was Sheriff Champ Wallace. Every man carried a gun. The sheriff had a pair. He put one in the ribs of Sherry and another in the stomach of Bill Garvin.

"Steady, Bill," said Sherry, seeing the grim features of his partner contract. "Steady . . . and get your hands up. The sheriff's having a little joke."

"Fan 'em," said the sheriff. He was a big, swollen-chested man with a red face, and his nerve was even bigger than his body. "Go through 'em, boys!"

They went through the two and put on the bar a small heap of tobacco sacks, cigarette papers, a pair of workman-like Colts, and finally two thick sheaves of paper money. It was the money that the sheriff bent his head above.

He had in one hand a list of numbers jotted on a card, and he kept nodding. Sherry, his hands almost touching the ceiling, understood what the nodding meant. There *had* been a man as big as Jumbo Joe at the robbing of the Overland. There had been Jumbo himself, and he had paid for the wet cattle with hot money. He had paid with greenbacks whose numbers were known and advertised.

Jack Sherry, looking down, saw the face of Bill Garvin pinched and withered with a sudden, fierce determination. There was no chance against such a crowd of armed men as this. He wanted to speak a word that would check the flaming madness in Garvin's eyes, but before he could utter a sound Garvin was at work. The sudden downward stroke of both arms knocked the nearest gun out of line with his body and that of Sherry. One of the weapons exploded. The roar of it reëchoed through the room. With a dropping fist, Sherry hit Sheriff Champ Wallace on the side of the head and crashed the officer into the wall.

Bill Garvin was already at the swing door to the street, and Sherry, fighting off two of the customers, bounded in pursuit. Garvin was through now, and Sherry was on the threshold when a bullet struck him in the back like a fist and sent him staggering into the open of the street.

Still he could run, though he was sure that he was carrying death with him. He saw Garvin turning the corner of the building into a lot covered with thick brush, and he dodged the corner in pursuit. He heard wild shouts of alarm, the running rush of booted feet behind. Half a dozen cowpunchers who were sauntering up the sidewalk turned through a shaft of lamplight and rushed at Garvin as Bill entered the brush.

Sherry strode for the point of contact. He saw the men spill all over Bill. He felt the brush whipping at his legs. That bullet had been tagged with his death, but if he could get to Garvin, his immense hands would give his partner a fighting chance for safety. Then another blow struck him from behind, a glancing clip across the head that dropped him face downwards into darkness.

Out of that darkness he wakened by degrees. There was such pain that he closed his eyes and tried to sink into unconsciousness once more. There was such pain that his face puckered like that of a child about to weep. His heart was pumping nausea and weakness. Thoughts would not come clearly, only wavering, flickering images that told him that Bill Garvin had been captured and that he, Jack Sherry, somehow in the darkness had remained

96

free. Free to die? Well, it's better to die in a hell of fire at the side of your partner than to live after deserting him.

Sherry kept thinking to himself: *They got Bill! Damn 'em, they got old Bill!*

The horror of that thought pulled him up on his hands and knees. The brush crackled. The pain was horrible. A branch slapped him wetly in the face. His own blood soaked the leaves. He looked up where the stars whirled in the sky above him. They had seen Bill Garvin taken.

But what was Bill thinking when he went down under the rush? As he struggled against long odds, had he looked vainly for his partner to come to his aid? One doubt of Bill had never entered Jack Sherry's brain since that day, years before, when Bill Garvin had dared the swirl of the Big Muddy, so far north, and brought Sherry, living, to the shore.

They'd caught Bill Garvin now, and blackness and bitterness must be in his heart as he lay handcuffed in the jail. He for the first time was doubting his partner. But he couldn't know that in the morning they would find that partner dead in the brush. The dogs would find him and howl till men came. And then the burning doubts of Bill Garvin would turn into sorrow.

He had to get to Bill Garvin quickly. Then, by God, the law could hang them together, side by side. He had to let Bill Garvin know at once that he had not deserted a lost cause.

Jack Sherry began crawling toward a light which shone faintly through the brush. It led him to a fence through which he crawled and, looking up, he saw a hitching rack with half a dozen horses tethered to it. That would be better. If he could get on one of those horses, he could ride to the jail more easily than he could crawl to it.

How quiet the town was! He could hear voices murmuring in the distance. He heard the small treble of laughter of a young child. Those people, living here, were not in pain. No man since the beginning of time had known what pain was — but Sherry knew. He had a belly full of it.

He took the nearest horse, crawled to it, gripped the stirrup, and pulled himself slowly to his feet, though he felt life ebbing from him with every breath. He thought he would faint at once when he was standing erect. He had to bow his head into the saddle and lean his weight. The horse turned its head and snuffled at him, blowing out its hot breath when it smelled Jack's blood.

The next effort would be the last. He used a hand to help lift his trembling knee and so got his foot into the stirrup. It was a vast labor. Then, three times, he heaved and swayed. But the power had gone out of those great arms. And only at the third effort would they drag Jack Sherry's body up and let him sprawl in the saddle.

He pulled on the reins. There was a spinning blackness across his eyes, but somehow he would find Bill Garvin and the jail. There must be a God in a heaven who sees to it that honest men reach their friends in time to die.

After a time he found that he was lying head down over the pommel of the saddle, his arms dangling on either side of the neck of the horse. He somehow realized a horrible fact. He had neglected to untie the lead rope.

Now, with a weak, trembling hand, he unknotted the rope. It flapped into the dust beneath the rack. Again he tried to push himself erect as he pulled at the reins, but the effort was too great. The horse, turning from the rack, plodded slowly at a walk up the street.

God! Was this the right direction? He could not tell. He was doing his best, and that was all he could manage. When he stared to the side, the rays of lamplight blurred as though his eyes were filled with tears. Then the sense went out of him.

Out of the town the horse continued at the same sedate, steady walk. It turned left off the road and took a trail. Here the going

98

was rougher, and the body of big Jack Sherry slid more and more to the side. It jolted down until he was half way to the ground. At last he fell. His foot caught in the stirrup. He was dragged a little distance before the foot disengaged. Then, face down, he lay senseless. The slow movement of the heavens lifted the stars out of the east. New constellations rose, but still the man remained motionless.

## II

## "ALONE WITH DEATH"

The dry, chill night wind fumbled at Jack Sherry's body, probed it, found tormented nerves, and tortured them still more, sending up into his brain a succession of jarring messages. At last the brain responded. It roused Sherry to pain, but a pain less great than that which had numbed his body before. He sat up with a mighty effort. It seemed that his life was pouring out of his breast.

"Old Bill!" he murmured.

It seemed to him, at that moment, that he was beside Bill Garvin. Then he was aware that the wilderness was around him. Thinking back, he remembered the town had spread around him and, above all he recalled the laughing voice of the child. He remembered the horse. His chin was scraped and so was his right hand. This was what made him realize what had happened. A certain awe came over him, with a feeling that this escape for him had been predestined, pre-arranged. If so, it was because in some manner he would be able to bring help to Bill Garvin.

He could remember another thing — that the money from the Overland robbery had been taken out of his own pockets by the sheriff, and therefore the blame fell directly on his head. They might find him guilty — but not Bill Garvin! Then, abruptly, Jack Sherry realized another thing. He was on a trail so dim that it could hardly be traveled once a month and that he had exactly nothing except the clothes he was dressed in — and a box of matches. His two hands and a box of matches — these were the tools with which he must save the dying flame of his life and bring himself back to strength — strength great enough to allow him to strike on behalf of Bill Garvin.

There was a pale rag of moon in the sky, but it gave him light enough. Sherry worked out of his coat, his shirt, his undershirt. He looked down at the big, gaping wound in his breast and shook his head. Plugged right in the back, as he was trying to get out of the saloon. That was where the bullet had torn its way out, and certainly it should have carried away his life with it. The whole front of him was dark with blood. When he moved, small wellings of blood oozed out of the mouth of the wound.

He used his teeth to chew through the hemmed margins of his undershirt. Then with teeth and hands he tore it into strips. He tied strips together to make a bandage. He laid a handful of dust over the bullet hole and bound the bandage closely about it.

He was thirsty. The sound of trickling water drew him, painfully crawling, until he came to the verge of a little runlet. The water was cold. It washed the taste of whiskey and blood and dust out of his mouth. He felt better. But he had to have food. Weariness and weakness came over him. He thought he was falling asleep. His eyes closed.

He awoke in the morning, feverish, very cold, and with a trembling weakness that shook him when he tried to move. He drank from the rivulet again, and again it gave him the blessing of hope. Somehow he would endure!

For three days and nights he lay, rarely moving except to drink from the stream. His pain diminished while his fever increased. Hunger gnawed at him till he was as worn by it as an old bone. But his brain was busy. The hills were full of rabbits and, on the fourth day, he began to devise the clumsiest figure-four traps that ever were seen. His tools were his hands and his teeth and strips of his clothing.

The clumsy traps were made and set slowly . . . slowly. He had to lie on his back most of the time. He had to shut his mind to Bill Garvin. His partner, by this time, was certain that Sherry had simply pulled out of the community and hidden his head like a coward. They were trying Bill Garvin for his life. The jury was finding him guilty. The judge was sentencing him to be hanged. Through these scenes Sherry's half-delirious imagination went racing as he painfully put together his traps.

That first day he caught a rabbit. He devoured it almost raw, savagely. He had never eaten food so good. Afterwards, he slept, slept so hard that, when he wakened, it seemed to him that he was in a new world, a kinder place for existence. For there was a warm stream of power running through his body.

Strength came back to him by degrees, day by day. He could crawl. He could take off the stained, encrusted bandage. He could sit up. And always there was a whip that scourged his soul, telling him that he must hurry, because Bill Garvin needed him. That was why he developed his strength with the most patient care. When his legs gave way, he would lie on the ground and use his arms in calisthenics to develop the wasted muscles.

But strength was coming. Like a plant it grew in him, forging tall, thrusting upwards, putting out branches. The blossoming of that strength would be the instant when he clasped the hand of Bill Garvin again.

He told himself that he was not fit to enter the world in which he would have to fight for Bill Garvin until he was able to run up the hill fifty yards to a certain black rock. And he could not run at all. Then, one day, he could make two or three springing paces. Then he was able to go fifteen yards. And then, after a long while, it was a bright, fresh morning and his knees held up while he ran all the way to the black rock. He sank down exhausted beside it. He held up his thin, gaunt arms to the sky.

What he said was simply: "Old Bill, I'm coming back!"

# III

## "OUT OF THE DARK VALLEY"

No stranger figure ever came down the trail. His coat was still fairly intact, but there was neither shirt nor undershirt beneath it. His trousers were worn to rags. His boots were parched and wrinkled but whole. When he looked down at himself, combing his beard with his fingers, he could not help smiling. That, perhaps, was as close as he would ever come to laughter in the course of his life to come. Each mile he sat down to rest. But he hit the sign of hoofs and wagon ruts at last.

He was sitting on a stone at the roadside when he heard hoofbeats. He did not try to hide. Thin, ragged, no one would know him now. Rapidly the sound of the horse's hoofs grew louder. And here came a girl with her head thrown back, the flash and the joy of the morning in her face. The loveliness of that face was food and drink to Jack Sherry. She was very close before he realized that it was Paula Carey. And she was nearly opposite him before her eyes focused on him.

She cried out when she noticed this gaunt, bearded, hollow-eyed apparition and, perhaps startled, she spurred her horse

102

ahead. The trees closed behind her, and she was gone. Jack Sherry felt a sudden feeling of security. People would not be able to recognize him.

Again the clinking of hoofs on the rocky road snapped him alert, and Paula Carey came into view again. At a short distance behind him, she stopped. Sherry stood up.

"You . . . you startled me," said the girl. "I wanted to come back to find out about you. You . . . look hungry."

"I am," he told her. Even his voice was altered. The old resonance had changed to a hoarse urgency.

She reached into a pocket of her blouse and brought out some bills.

"I haven't much money with me," she said, "but you're welcome to it." She flushed. "You see, I don't carry any food on me, and town's not so far away. There's a middling poor restaurant. . . ."

"I'm not hungry for anything better than rabbit meat," he answered.

She seemed on the verge of throwing the money to him. Then, staring into his hollow, brilliant eyes, she forced the mustang ahead and leaned forward in the saddle, placing the bills in his bony hand. Sherry knew she hated to do this. Her face was pale, strained.

"Why are you afraid, Paula?" he asked. His lips twisted wryly.

She gasped as she heard her name. "Do you know me? Who are you?"

He shook his head. "Just an *hombre* with a price on his head," he told her.

She slipped off her horse and stood before him. "There's something about you that I almost recognize," she said. "If you'll trust me, I want to help." Then, almost as an afterthought, she said in a very small thin voice: "Jack, I trust you."

"Law-abiding people shouldn't have anything to do with

103

hunted men," he said.

"If you know me, you won't talk like that," said the girl, and she stared at his bearded face as though trying to peer through a fog.

He held out the money she had given to him. "Would you give away your last cent to a tramp, Paula?" he asked. "Hell, I can't use your money. I'm not a beggar."

"I won't take it back. Give it to any man who needs it more than you do."

"By God, you're as grand a girl as I thought!" said Sherry.

She came still closer. "You've been sick, and you're still sick. Tell me about yourself."

His mouth tightened. "It would only drag you into trouble." Then he smiled under his beard. "Paula, you couldn't help throwing yourself into a lost cause, could you?"

"Well," she exclaimed impatiently, "will you tell me what you're going to do?"

He watched her, and it seemed to Sherry a horrible thing that time should ever touch her and remodel in shadow this brightness of beauty. Trouble could show in her eyes only. Her lips could never help smiling a little. But life would give her agonies to endure. She would lie gaping in the darkness, her teeth showing, gripped hard together, her eyes rolling, searching for mercy or for help. Pain, it flashed upon Sherry, is like salt in bread: a necessary part of living — but he wanted to keep it from her.

"I want to talk to you. That's all," said Sherry. "I want to tell you that to see you is enough to make a sick man well. There's nothing cruel or mean or savage or selfish about you."

"You don't know me, if you say that," answered the girl. "Don't talk about me. Talk about yourself. Talk . . . !" She paused, then: "There is some true, real purpose in your mind."

"Why do you say that?"

"Because you have the look of a man who is seeing the distance

104

. . . and climbing the mountains of it."

Again he smiled rather bitterly. "I have a friend in trouble, and I want to help him. That's the only purpose I have."

"Who?" she insisted.

He hesitated. If he revealed the name, he might be revealing himself. Yet he hungered mightily to learn the news of what had happened to Bill Garvin.

"His name is Garvin," said Sherry. And there was a touch of defiance in his voice. "Ever hear of him?"

"Bill Garvin? Then you *are* Jack Sherry!" she cried. "Jack, Jack, where have you been? They found the bloody trail where you'd fallen in the brush. Jack, Jack, you've been dying all this time!"

She took his gaunt hands under the pits of her arms and put her own hands on his shoulders, reaching up. He could feel the warmth and the softness of her body and the rapid throbbing of the life in it. She was only so much flesh and blood. And yet there was a touch of divinity added, like perfume to a flower, or music to the wind.

"Never mind me. What about Bill?" asked Sherry. "Will you tell me about him?"

"Tell me first what you've been doing."

"Laying low like a hunted animal. But I'm all right now."

Tears filled her eyes as she stared up at him. She shook her head. "I . . . I can't tell you about Garvin."

"He's gone then," said Sherry dully. "They've tried him, sentenced him, and hanged him."

"No, no! But they've tried and sentenced him."

"Where is he now?"

"In the penitentiary."

"Ah," muttered Sherry with a great sigh of relief. "Only that?" Then it seemed as if something had struck him like a physical blow, though he didn't exactly know why or how. "Come out

105

with it!" he demanded.

"He's in the death house," she said at last.

Sherry stared at the ground. "Go on," he said. "Tell me how it happened."

"There was no chance for Bill," she answered gently. "Father and I testified about seeing Bill on the Mexican side of the river with the cattle. We tried to make it appear that you and he couldn't have been in the During Gulch at the Overland hold-up. But that was no good. There would have been time for hard riders to get away after the hold-up of the train. The district attorney declared that the robbers would have done just that . . . take their money and buy contraband beef with some of it. He made it part of his story to damn Bill Garvin when it came to his summing up."

"Besides your father and you, did Bill have a friend?"

"No. There's a sort of singleness about Bill. He couldn't have more than one friend at a time, I suppose. . . . We talked to him in jail."

"Did he ask about me?"

She paused. "No," she said. "But we told him about the blood-stained place in the brush where it seemed that you must have fallen. We told him about the horse found covered with blood out at the Rand ranch, back in the hills."

"He didn't say anything to that?"

"No. He wouldn't say a word about you, Jack."

"Why should he?" asked Sherry bitterly. "Hanging won't mean much to Bill if he thinks I've walked out on him. If he thinks that I'm yellow, a quitter, he'll be through . . . ready to cash in his chips."

"He sat like a stone all through the trial," she said. "They had to repeat questions to him three times before he seemed to understand. And then he answered the first thing that came into his mind. If he had a case, he would have thrown it away.

But it isn't your fault. Don't look as though *you* had hurt him, Jack!"

He stood up again. The look of him made her shrink.

"What are you going to do?" she asked.

"Something that needs doing," he answered quietly.

"You'll let father and me help you?"

"What I must do, I must do by myself, alone," he answered. Then, after a pause, he added: "Except that I'll have the thought of you along with me, day and night."

# IV

## "OUTLAW BARGAIN"

The hole-in-the-wall country around Travis Junction was famous for the number of outlaws that lurked in it. The rough maze of *coulées* and up-and-down terrain brought the outlaws, and the outlaws brought Jake Myers, the lawyer. He followed them as a buzzard follows dying animals. He was keen as a bird to pick up his profits wherever he could find them. He liked capital cases. He liked criminals, slick ones — men who could kill and rob and leave no legal proof of their foulness. He had an instinct so profound that he was able to tell within five hundred dollars the sum which he would need to collect from the friends and supporters of the endangered crook. Jake Myers could hang a jury on some small, insignificant technicality, and he passed out his bribes with such discretion that no one ever could follow the trail of his crooked dealing. His influence extended far underground, like the roots of the mesquite.

Jake, all day long, used to sit behind closed doors. At night he ventured to smoke a cigar, sitting on the front porch of his house. It was a very good cigar. And after dark was the only time he permitted himself to use fine tobacco, for he dreaded lest someone should discover that he was rich — that his house stood over a mine of gold that, every year, grew deeper and deeper. During the day his talk was always of his poverty while his claws continually raked in more gold.

On this night the thoughts of Jake Myers were peculiarly sweet, and there was clamped between his teeth a thick perfecto whose richness made amends for the rank little stogies with which he had to content himself during the day. Even then he felt uncomfortable. More so when out of the darkness a figure loomed and walked up the steps. Jake Myers pulled up the short, sawed-off shotgun that always gave composure to his nerves. He held the weapon across his knees in both hands.

"Who's there?" he asked.

"One of the boys who's going to be a friend of yours," said the tall shadow.

"What is your name?"

"Jack Sherry."

"Well, well, well," murmured Jake Myers, and his grin was so wide that it brought his long nose and his long chin close together. "Glad to meet you, Jack. How's things with you since you left During Gulch?" He threw that in to show that he was in touch with the affair.

Instead of making answer, Sherry demanded: "When does Bill Garvin hang?"

"In five days," said Myers. That was correct.

"He can't hang in five days," answered Sherry tonelessly.

"Who says he can't?"

"I do."

"Yes? It'd cost twenty-five hundred to stay that execution."

"All right. I'll get you the twenty-five hundred."

"Good boy," said the lawyer. "I can see you're not the sort

to let down a friend." He allowed the shotgun to slide into its place of rest. The huge shadowy form drew closer to him.

"Sit down," urged Myers. "There's a chair right near me. And tell me how things are going since you got rich?"

"I never was rich."

"Sixty thousand's big. Or is that just change to you?"

"I didn't stick up the Overland at During Gulch. Bill and I didn't have any part of it."

"Somebody wished that coin into your pockets, eh?" sneered Myers.

"Jumbo Joe and his partner, Tex Walton, paid us that seven thousand for wet cattle," said Sherry. "What'll it cost to buy Bill Garvin out of the prison?"

"Hold on!" exclaimed Myers. "You can't buy a man out of the death house. You can't buy pardons in this state."

"Not even if I had the money?"

"Brother," said Myers, "you're talking out of your class now. It would take five, six, seven thousand, maybe. It depends on how they stand . . . the boys that hold down the key jobs."

"You know them all by their first names?"

"I know them by their first names, all right. And it costs me some money to know that much. But they're not in the bag till they're put in place for every job. Besides, it would take me some time . . . two days . . . to find out the details."

"I'll be back here two days from tonight."

"I'll want a little token payment," said Myers.

"You can't have it. I need two days to dig up the cash."

"I'd like to oblige you," whined Myers, "but these are hard times. How is a poor man like me to find twenty-five hundred that he can pass up to the big fellows?"

"Dig in your cellar and maybe you'll strike it rich," said Sherry.

The suggestion brought the lawyer out of his chair. "Dig in my cellar?" he gasped. "What d'you mean?"

"You don't use a bank, so you probably bury your cash in a hole in the ground, and a rat like you wouldn't trust any ground away from your own place," said Sherry. "Get that stay of execution. I'll be back here in two days with some money for you."

"Who talked to you about my cellar?" cried Myers. "There ain't a thing in my cellar. I'm as poor as the devil."

Sherry grinned. "So long, Myers," he said.

He turned and strode across the steps. As he faded into the darkness, he could hear a groaning behind him. That was Myers in agony of fear and grief for his buried treasure.

But it was not the dirty money or Myers's fear that Sherry had in mind. He had to fill his hands with eight or ten thousand dollars in order to buy the lawyer, and he was reasonably sure where that money might be located. It would be hard to find, and dangerous, but once in his hands it would bring Bill Garvin a long stride nearer to liberty.

Across country sloped Sherry with the night wind cold against his face. He headed for a small ranch house about five miles from Travis Junction. Behind the ranch house arose a hill with a brush-covered top, and it was in that brush that Sherry stretched himself and slept in utter exhaustion. With the first glimmering of the dawn he was awake and looking down the hill on the little house with its ragged cluster of sheds and its tangles of outlying corrals.

It was the middle of the morning before he saw a man issue from the kitchen door, light a cigarette, and go into a corral where he snagged a running horse with the first cast of his rope. That was probably Tex Walton, almost as famous with a rope as with a gun.

It was Tex Walton, certainly, because after the mustang was saddled and mounted and merely humped its back towards bucking, the rider gave it a severe beating with his quirt. Sherry could see the flash of the whip and hear the smart crack of it

110

against the body of the horse. Then Walton shot his beaten horse down the road towards the town.

An hour later the towering, heavy form of Jumbo Joe appeared. Even in the distance the deformed twist of his face was clearly to be seen. He went into a shed and brought out a huge stallion capable of carrying his bulk. Slowly he jogged the animal away.

Sherry stole down the hill and into the house. There had been sixty thousand dollars in loot taken from the Overland. It was hardly probable that the two killers had squandered all that money in such a short time. Rather, they were ones to make a big haul grow into still bigger dimensions by carefully investing it in other goods — like wet cattle from Mexico.

Where could they keep their treasure? Never in a bank, of course. A more likely spot was a hole in the ground. Or under a floorboard. Or in some recess of a wall. Sherry went over every floorboard in the single-story shack. Not one of them was loose; not one was held by nails from whose heads the rust had been knocked by recent hammering. After that he gave his attention to the walls, but not a suspicious cranny could he find.

There were other places. The whole house was a dirty litter of boxes and harness and saddles and fishing-tackle and guns. So much the better for Sherry. Deep in his heart he knew that these men deserved killing, and he was determined to have the killing of them. This household confusion made the search more difficult. He had to go through the battered old trunks in the bedroom, through the bedding, probing the mattresses, squeezing the pillows. In every case he had to be sure that he left everything exactly as he had found it.

Finally, when it was afternoon, he went down into the cellar. It consisted of only two rooms, and the light was so dim that he had to use sense of touch almost as much as his eyes. He tapped the walls. He examined the floor, making sure that there were no soft spots where the earth might have been moved.

He discovered a small mound, but it was of firmly compacted ground that could not have been disturbed recently. In short, he was convinced that wherever the treasure of Jumbo and Tex Walton was hid, it was not in the house.

Just as that conviction came over him, he heard the sudden beating of hoofs towards the ranch house. He looked accusingly towards the slanted rays of sunshine that crossed the cellar and proved the sun to be hardly half way towards the western horizon. He had not expected the pair back before night. Now, if he attempted to get out, they would run him down in a moment. He pulled out a cedar-handled Colt and held it in a steady hand.

# V

## "BLOOD MONEY"

He could hear the corral gate creak on its hinges and the jangle of spurs. Then the steps of the men were loud on the floor of the shack. The impacts knocked out little showers of dust over his head that brightened in the rays of slanting sun. Every word spoken came clearly to him.

He squatted on the hummock of hard earth and waited. He had learned patience. He had learned it so well while he lay hiding out, helpless and bullet-pierced, that now he felt no nervousness — only the dull ache of the healed wound that had penetrated his body. It reminded him his life had been spared, and such miracles had to be for a purpose. The purpose was clear: he must wipe out Jumbo Joe and Tex Walton.

They were talking of a cattle deal and cursing and laughing at someone they had gulled. They had sold him cattle in the morning and stampeded and stolen them back in the night of the same day. They talked of a girl that Tex desired.

"She wants me to marry her," said Tex, "and what the hell do you think of that?"

They both laughed in long derision.

"The girls don't bother me none," declared Jumbo Joe.

"You don't bother them neither," said Tex Walton.

"I ain't a fool, throwing away my time and hard cash on 'em," answered Jumbo.

"Talk to 'em, Jumbo," said Tex. "That's all they want . . . talk!"

"I used to see Handsome Jack Sherry, as the girls called him . . . I used to see him gibberin' and grinnin' with the girls," said Jumbo, "and it used to gripe me. That's when I started to hate him. I'd rather be damned than caught makin' eyes at any fool girl."

"He ain't makin' eyes at the girls now," commented Tex Walton. "I wonder what became of him?"

"He dropped off the back of that Rand horse into the river. Where else would he drop to?" asked Jumbo Joe. "Take those sacks of canned chuck down into the cellar. They're in the way up here."

"Take care of 'em yourself," said Walton.

Footfalls immediately overhead made the words unintelligible for a moment. Then the trap door of the cellar was flung back with a crash, and a huge pair of legs descended — Jumbo Joe came into view, with the weight of a great sack in his arms, and behind him came Tex Walton. Sherry told himself that he could do it now. There *was* a controlling destiny that guided him here where he could take them at a disadvantage. His own eyes, accustomed to the dimness of the cellar light, allowed him to see them clearly. But they, as their fumbling steps showed, could see almost nothing.

113

Standing in the corner, Sherry took good aim at the twisted face of Jumbo. His finger pressed the trigger. Then he discovered that he could not fire! This was murder. Even though there was justice behind him and even though he was executing the true will of the law, he could not shoot. He was amazed. An awe grew coldly up in Jack Sherry.

Only if he were seen could he fire — but he was not seen. They merely threw down their jangling burdens and passed back up the stairs with Tex saying: "We wanta lay in a lot more of this stuff before winter."

Then they were above in the kitchen, rattling at the stove, still knocking the thin showers of dust out of the floorboards as they stalked about. A faint smell of cookery reached down even into the cellar and made Sherry's mouth water. But again he sat down upon the mound of the hard cellar earth and waited patiently.

If his hand had been held, what power had restrained it? Was there, after all, a Judge who watched men on earth and brought them to justice in mysterious ways? Above him, two robbers and murderers were reveling in the fullness of their lives. He sat in the damp of the cellar gloom and felt the pinch of hunger and the long despair of his friend who waited in the death house. But in the end there might be justice done.

Having eaten, they were leaving the house again and going down into the south-eastern quarter section, they said, to bring up some fresh saddle horses. He waited until they had left the house, and the noise of them had faded. Then he passed up the cellar stairs. He needed food. There was not a chance in a thousand that they would miss a thick chunk off that side of bacon or a portion of flour out of the sack which sat on the floor surrounded by a white aura of dust. He took the two necessaries and ventured outside.

The sun was blazing low in the west. The air was already

114

freshening towards the night coolness. Yonder the hill was waiting for him like a perch for a watching bird. He climbed back to his watching post and stretched himself again in the brush. Not till dark would he venture to light a fire to cook his food.

He saw the day grow old. In the distance two shadowy riders were rounding up horses, bringing them back towards the house. Coming out of the shadow of the valley, the mustangs flashed like metal in the last of the sunlight. They were enclosed in a corral. They gathered into it like an explosion, the dust of their stamping flying high overhead, rosily stained by the sunset. And so the day darkened, and the movements of all things below the hill were lost to him.

Still he could not relax his vigil, for it might be that one of the pair would come out with a lantern later on and reveal what he wanted to know by the place to which he went. Not until the light in the house was extinguished did Sherry turn to his cookery, and then stretch himself in sleep.

He was stronger, much stronger. His starved body ate up nourishment as a dry desert drinks water. His pinched muscles were starting to swell with strength. He was beginning to recognize himself, except when his fingers touched his face and felt the skin drawn so tight over the bones.

Dawn came again. The sun was not yet up when he saw the gleam of a light in the kitchen of the ranch house. The sun had barely begun to shine on the wheel of the windmill when the two came from the house, caught up horses, and departed, perhaps to sell once more what they had already sold and stolen back. That herd, Sherry guessed, was the same lot of wet cattle that he and Bill Garvin had brought across the border.

The day grew hot. Heat and brightness drowned the hills. Sweat dripped from the body of the patient watcher. He was half sleeping in the late afternoon before the two riders raised a dust on the distant road that wound towards the town, came out of the cloud, and unsaddled their horses in the corral. It would be dark before long, utterly dark, and Sherry's heart sank in him. For five days had been the apportioned time Bill Garvin had in the death house and, unless Jake Myers had been willing to work for nothing in the beginning, no stay of the execution would be put through.

In three days Bill Garvin would hang, while Sherry still waited on the top of the hill, like a hawk in the sky, trying to spy out the secret of Jumbo and Tex Walton. In two days he had promised to return to the lawyer with the money. The second day was already closing.

The sun sank. The crimson fire rushed upwards across the sky. Light began to fade from the zenith and darken around the edges of the horizon. Then Jumbo Joe came out of the house, crossed to the windmill, and stood there for a moment, slowly turning his body as he scanned all things around him. So a beast of prey might have come out of its den and regarded the landscape before it set about uncovering a treasure of buried meat. That comparison entered the mind of Sherry with a great shock. Eagerly he strained his eyes and saw Jumbo pull down the lever that drew the wheel of the windmill out of the breeze and locked it. As it oscillated for a moment, he heard the rusted machinery groaning. It was a sound of almost human complaint out of the distance. Then he could see, very dimly through the thickening of the dusk, how Jumbo Joe kneeled and seemed to be lifting the top section of the well casing. The giant remained there for only a short time then hurried back to the house. The kitchen door opened. The huge figure was outlined for an instant against the light. Then the door shut behind.

Jack Sherry came down the hill at a run. Twice he stumbled and fell because he was by no means sure of his knees. When he came closer to the house, he heard the clanking of the windmill and the rushing sound of its wheel long before he could see its gaunt frame. Now he stood inside the square of the big upright timbers. They trembled with the working of the pump. The water gushed into a long tin funnel and ran away with a resonant murmur until it fell with a resounding plump into the trough. With every stroke of the pump this cadence of the rushing water began and faded a little to be renewed by another pulse.

It was dangerous to pull the wheel out of the wind, because the cessation of the noise might be noticed at once in the house. However, Sherry pulled down the lever, and the fan and the wheel, in two gestures, drew groaningly together. Breathing short, looking back over his shoulder towards the light in the kitchen window, Sherry slipped the lever under its catch. A moment later he had shifted the pump casing away from that of the wall and tried the upper section of the latter. The cold, wet metal yielded instantly to his pressure upwards. A section came free, and his hand was instantly down the circular muzzle of the well.

He found what he wanted at once — the coarseness of tarpaulin touching his fingers a foot or so down the shaft. He pulled out a small bundle, laid it on the ground, and fitted the lower casing in place. He wanted to flee then, but he felt that to leave the windmill out of whack would be to call the two robbers after him at once, so he delayed to fasten the pump casing once more to that of the well. He had barely accomplished this when a dim gesture of light waved towards him from the house. The door of the kitchen was open. Tex Walton was saying, as he stood in the doorway: "Why didn't you turn the pump on again when you got through?"

"I did," answered the rumbling voice of Jumbo.

"You're cock-eyed," observed Walton. "There's plenty of air movin', and the windmill's tied up."

Jack Sherry moved away into the darkness, stepping very softly, very slowly. That dim lamp shine seemed to him brighter than noonday, because bullets might fly down the course of it at any time. He reached a wide bush and crouched for a moment behind it, breathing hard, the tarpaulin crushed between his elbow and his ribs. Behind him, he heard the windmill squeak, then the throbbing vibration of the pump as Tex Walton loosed the wheel to the wind.

# VI

## "THE TEST OF A MAN"

Out of the darkness once more a tall, shadowy form loomed near the front porch of Jake Myers where the lawyer marked his position by the glow of his cigar. When he drew in a long puff, the sheen of the living coal dimly illumined his ugly face. So his picture alternated between ghostliness and dark death.

"Hello, Jake," said Sherry. "What's up?"

"You could see in the papers," answered Myers. "I get a two-week stay for Bill Garvin. Without a penny in my hand, I get that execution date pushed backward. Now, does it prove that Jake Myers is a friend of the poor boys who're in trouble?"

"I'm paying you money," said Sherry. "Go inside the house."

They went inside. Myers, after lighting a lamp, shadowed his face with one hand and looked at the emaciated features of Sherry.

"You are a sick man, Sherry," said the lawyer. "You are almost a dying man."

Sherry was holding out his hand. It was difficult for him to shake the hand of Myers. He would as soon have shaken the claw of an eagle but, when he remembered that this fellow had connived two extra weeks of life for his partner, a great rush of emotion beat down all his prejudices. The ugly little lawyer, staring up into the starved face of Sherry, took the hand and grinned. He seemed to understand perfectly.

"You love a friend!" he said. "But, if you like him so much, what money have you brought for him?"

"Here," said Sherry, "is the twenty-five hundred I promised for the stay of execution." He tossed a packet of wrapped money on the table. It was instantly opened. A tremor shook the hands of Jake Myers as he counted the sheaf of bills. His whole body was trembling with joy.

"Sherry," he said, "you are a noble young man. God is kind to people who keep promises."

"But Garvin is in the death house," said Sherry. "What's the next step for getting him out?"

Myers wrinkled his face. "Have you money for that also?" he asked.

"I have," said Sherry.

Myers groaned. "My God, how I want to help you. But there is no way."

"There's got to be a way," declared Sherry.

"There is no way," answered Myers. "I can have the south gate of the prison opened at night. I can make the two guards on the wall turn their backs . . . or shoot crooked. I can open the inner door of the prison also. I can even send hacksaw blades into the death house in the food from the kitchen, but I can't bribe the devil who is the guard in that place. Two jailers, both devils. One for the day and one for the night. Money will not buy them. All they want is a chance to see their prisoners hanged. They are like coyotes. Dead things please them, and that is why they were chosen as guards for the death house."

"Send in the saw blades, and that isn't enough," agreed Sherry. "Bill Garvin isn't a clever fighting man."

"If he tried to escape," Myers said, "he would only be shot down. His hands are empty, and one of these two devils is always on the watch."

"Two men would have ten times the chances of one," said Sherry.

"There is no other man in the death house," answered Jake Myers. He shrugged his shoulders and extended his hands, palms up. "You see, it is impossible? I have tried everything, thought of everything. There is no way."

"There is still one," suggested Sherry. "We could send a man into the death house to fight a way out with Bill."

"Send a man in . . . ?" began the lawyer. Then he broke into a hearty laughter, as though he had found a touch of comedy that he could really appreciate. "Yes, yes," he said. "By all means find a man ready to be condemned to death and sent into the death house. Find a man like that, and then he and Bill Garvin might have one chance in five. Not more! Only try to find me a man like that, my young friend." Myers began to laugh again, but something in the still, white face of Sherry stopped him. "What do you mean by staring at me?" asked the lawyer. "You? Would you go to prison yourself? Would you sit in the death house for the sake of dying with him? You would have only one chance in five, one chance in ten. For God's sake, what are you thinking of?"

"All the rest," said Sherry, "the bribing of the guards, the opening of the gates . . . how much will that cost?"

"Eight thousand," said Myers. "And it is so cheap only because I throw in my own services for nothing."

Sherry grinned faintly at the little man. He knew perfectly that at least half of the total amount would end in the pocket of Jake Myers himself.

"Here's a part of eight thousand," he said. And taking out a deep sheaf of bills, he counted out five thousand dollars and dropped that on the table. "You get the other three when Bill Garvin and I are out of the pen. Is that fair?"

The startled eyes of Myers peered after the treasure that remained unspent and was disappearing into the pocket of Sherry again. "But all that other money . . . where will you put it when you go to risk your life in the prison, Sherry? But no, you cannot go."

"They'll send me for the same hold-up and shooting that sent up Bill," suggested Sherry.

"They won't do that," answered Myers. "If Bill dies, that will be a life for a life. The district attorney will be satisfied with that . . . I know him. No, they would not hang you also. They have one victim for that hold-up of the Overland, and that is enough. They would never send you to join Bill Garvin in the death house."

"They'll send me there for a second killing, though," said Sherry.

"Hey?" exclaimed the lawyer.

"If a second killing is needed to put me with Bill," said Sherry, "that's what I'm going to do, and I'll do it now."

"Wait!" shouted the other.

But Sherry had already strode out into the night.

It was the brightest and the hottest part of the next afternoon when Tex Walton stepped into Mallon's saloon. Outside the swing doors, the day glimmered like a white furnace. Even inside the shadow of the saloon, sweat constantly beaded foreheads. Where the poker players sat in a corner, there was so little air that the men were sweating through the shoulders of their flannel shirts, and big black arcs appeared under the pits of their arms.

Tex Walton, glancing over all these faces with the wary eye of one who has a past that may overtake him at any moment, was startled by the very pale, thin, handsome features of a man in the farthest corner. A sudden thrill of expectancy made the head of Walton jerk up.

"You?" he called. "Who are you?" He pointed, using his left

hand. The right remained close to the holstered gun on his thigh.

That tall man in the corner with the thin, pale face remained seated for a moment before he rose and stood, tall as a giant.

"Take another look, Tex," he said. "If you don't remember my face, you might remember my voice. I've come for you, Tex."

"You've what? Who in hell are you?"

"I'm Jack Sherry," said the big man. "Fill your hand!"

A startled, wordless sound of shock and excitement came from every throat in the room as men swung to see what happened. It looked to everyone like an almost even draw. The double report beat into the strained ears. The wisps of smoke curled small and thin from the muzzles of the guns. But then Tex Walton was seen to lean forward as though he were stooping to pick something from the floor. He reached still farther. The gun fell with a sudden rattle. His whole length smote the boards and knocked up a wide puff of dust. No one moved. Only Jack Sherry was stepping, without haste, towards the swing doors of the saloon with the gun naked in his hand.

"I'll be seeing you," he said at the doors and stepped out onto the street.

The silence behind him remained palpable and solid. It would shatter into action before too long, he knew, and there was still one thing he had to do before he gave himself into the hands of the law. He took the first horse at the hitching rack in front of Mallon's, a heavily-built roan, and on that horse galloped straight out of Travis Junction. He was at the outskirts of the town before he heard the outcry begin. He was well out on the road before the beating of rapid hoofs rolled from the town in pursuit.

Paula Carey, on these white-hot afternoons, used to leave the

122

breathless little ranch house and stretch in a hammock that was hung beneath a great fig tree. It was the only fig tree within a hundred miles, and its immense canopy of green was a famous landmark. The huge leaves made on the ground a big design of black with little quivering lines of sunshine between. She was between sleep and waking when she heard the hurried beating of the hoofs of a horse. She saw the rider then, with the dust cloud speeding back from the hoofs of his roan and rising and spreading into a cloud. Far back, there was another and much larger cloud puffing white against the sky.

The first rider, pulling his horse sharply to the side, ran it right at the low fence that enclosed a small alfalfa patch watered by the overflow from the water tank. The mustang reared, took the fence winging, and galloped straight on towards the fig tree, throwing high in the air clots of the soft alfalfa ground. Not until this instant did Paula Carey recognize Sherry.

The rumbling of the distant hoofs was growing louder as she sprang from the hammock to meet him and saw him slide down from the saddle. He threw his hat on the ground. He gave her not even a greeting as he thrust a wrapped-up bit of tarpaulin into her hands.

"Paula," he said, "there's eleven thousand dollars in stolen money inside of this. I took it from Jumbo and Tex Walton. They took it from the Overland. I'm going to prison. You're to keep this for me till I get out again."

The words struck her white, but her eyes did not waver. They grew bigger with faith and pity. He knew then that this moment would be stained indelibly into his memory. She was drawn into his mind as close as though he held her in his arms. Love was what he wanted to speak to her. Love was what strained in his throat. But there was another need greater than his, and that was the need of Bill Garvin in the death house. Every word he spoke must be for his friend.

She was gripping the tarpaulin hard between her hands. Then, turning, she thrust it under the light woolen throw which lay in the hammock. "I'll keep it as safe as though it were honest money," she said, facing him again. "Prison?" she pointed towards the approaching cloud of dust through which the figures of the riders could now be seen. "Right behind the house my own horse is standing. He'll carry you, Jack. Take him if the roan is spent. Quickly! You can still get away."

"I want them to catch me," answered Sherry. "Tex Walton is dead in Mallon's saloon. I shot him."

She could not grow whiter, but he waited to see horror come into her eyes. Instead, there was the same unwavering brightness.

"I'm going to the death house to bring out Bill Garvin," he said. "No matter what happens after this . . . even if they hang me . . . remember that I'm telling you the truth now. Bill Garvin and I didn't do the Overland job in During Gulch. Bill has to be set free. For the work that's going to be done, money will have to be paid. I've put that money in your hands. The moment that you hear Bill and I are out, Jake Myers, the crooked lawyer, will come to you. Give him this package . . . the moment you know that we're out of prison."

"I'll keep it till then," she said. "No one shall have it."

With a rushing of hoofs, with a shouting, the men from Travis Junction stormed up to the Carey ranch. They dismounted behind the fence. They vaulted over it and ran across the alfalfa. But instead of finding a fighting outlaw, they discovered the tall man and the girl standing quietly together.

The sheriff came first. He laid his gun against the ribs of Sherry and said: "Put up your hands, Sherry! There's going to be a hanging for this second job."

Sherry merely smiled at the girl and she, in some manner, was able to smile back at him. There was no need of the words that he had wanted to speak. Something passed between them, from eye to eye and from soul to soul. Later, Jack Sherry was still faintly smiling when the door of the jail clanged behind him.

# VII

## "A GAME WITH DEATH"

The lawyer, who was assigned to Sherry's defense by the judge, made a very good speech when he summed up his client's case, but they found Sherry guilty and sentenced him to be hanged by the neck until he was dead. When he had received the sentence, he turned — men were to remember this afterwards — and looked straight back across the courtroom to the place where Paula Carey was sitting. She stood up and, before the eyes of everyone there, she smiled back at him. There was no word spoken between them, but the whole town of Travis Junction knew what that smile meant. It knocked the brightness out of life for at least a score of young fellows, and every one of them was glad that the hangman was going to stretch the neck of Sherry.

It was that same evening, in the carelessly run jail, that big Jumbo Joe leaned against the bars of Sherry's cell and talked to him in a deep-throated murmur. "Sherry, I found out what you done at my ranch. I found signs in the soft of the ground under the windmill. There ain't another man likely to have feet long and narrow like yours. And there ain't another that would be takin' strides to match yours neither. You were out there, and you got the stuff, didn't you?"

Sherry confessed cheerfully: "Sure, I took the money, Jumbo."

"How'd you know that it was there?" asked Jumbo with no

apparent animosity. "This business of Tex don't make no difference to me. Tex was a damned fool. Woman crazy was what he was. So he got plastered with lead finally, and it was a kid like you that done him in. To hell with him! But what about that money you got from the well?"

"I've spent part, and I'm holding part," answered Sherry.

"How much have you spent?" asked Jumbo wistfully.

"About eight thousand."

Jumbo closed his eyes. His face was a mask of twisting pain for a moment. "Eight thousand gone," he sighed. "Eight thousand gone to the same hell that Tex is in. But where's the rest? There's more'n eleven thousand left after that."

"It's put away safe," said Sherry.

"Well, then, gimme an idea where to look for that cash, will you?"

"It's Overland money?" asked Sherry.

The big man squinted at him. "What d'you care where it came from? Where it come from don't count alongside of where it is right now," said Jumbo.

"I'm not talking about where it is," said Sherry.

"You ain't, eh? Listen, kid. You think I'm bluffing, but you're wrong. I'll split this here jail open like a nut and shell you out of it, if you say the word."

"When I'm out and free, Jumbo," said Sherry, "you and I are going to fight it out together. You understand that?"

He walked up close to the bars of his cell. Such a rage burned in him that he trembled as a flame trembles in the wind. The vast face of Jumbo changed color.

"You dummy," he said. "Would you rather be hanged than turned free? To hell with you then! If some way you should slip away from the law, look out for Jumbo. I got twenty thousand reasons for smashing you like a rotten apple and, by God, any one of those reasons is twice bigger than I need."

126

That was how Jumbo Joe left the jail, with the long spurs slashing from his heels, and his hat pulled far down over his eyes. He was gone from the mind of Sherry instantly. Nothing but Bill Garvin existed now. Only in the dim future might there be a chance to think about Jumbo again.

Three days later Mickey Duveen pushed open the steel door of the death house of the state prison and ushered the new prisoner down the aisle. It was not like an ordinary floor of a jail. The whole place was brighter. The windows were bigger and so were the thick bars that checkered the sunshine. The cells themselves were as large as rooms, and they were furnished with tables and chairs, for the last hours of a man were to be made comfortable in this place.

"Here you are," said Mickey Duveen, who was one of the two special guards of the death house, chosen because he loved this post above all others. "Here you are in your last hotel. You better enjoy it, kid."

As he spoke, he laughed with great relish. His head was very small. There was only one large feature in his face, and that was his mouth; wherefore his laughter seemed to swallow the rest of his face. He looked like an open red gullet on top of a thick pair of shoulders. Pausing at the second cell, he unlocked the door of it and jerked it open.

"The two of you oughta keep good company together," he declared, "because you're gonna hang on the same day."

He assisted tall Jack Sherry through the door with a thrust of his foot, but Sherry hardly felt the kick or heard the laughter. His eyes were too busy pouring over the face of Bill Garvin. It was strangely set in new lines of pain. It was thin and pale. It was as ugly a face as a man could find in a week's ride, but it looked to Sherry better than any vision of heaven.

They gripped hands. They were silent. They could order what

they wanted for food. It was the privilege of the death house. When they demanded roast chicken for that first evening meal, the little skewers which were thrust through the bird turned out to be small saw blades of the most perfect make.

It was Bill Garvin's logical brain that announced they would never be able to escape, even after his friend had murmured to him all the plans of Jake Myers. "There's only one thing for us to do," said Bill Garvin, "and that's to cut our way through the bars. But there's only about one hour a night when we could work because, except for about an hour in the dogwatch, one of the guards is always walking up and down the aisle. Suppose that we use every minute of that hour, each night . . . we can't cut through those bars in five sessions like that. And six days from this we hang. Jack, you been a fool again. You've throwed yourself away. You've throwed good money after bad."

Sherry closed his eyes and, against the dark of his mind, he saw the lovely face of Paula Carey. But Bill Garvin must not know about her. "No matter what happens," said Sherry, "it's got to happen to us together. You know that, Bill. So why keep on arguing? If we pull through, that's fine. If we smash, that's the best we can do."

Bill Garvin thought a long, silent moment. At last he said: "Being partners is a damn queer thing, Jack, ain't it?"

"Damned queer," agreed Sherry, and that was the end of their philosophizing on the subject of their reunion and their escape. From that moment they were constantly at work during every odd moment with the blades. They pulled the table over to the bars and sat there for hours during the day, apparently playing cards while either Mickey Duveen or Jeff Bender stalked up and down the aisle with shotgun on shoulder. But whenever the back of the guard was turned, or whenever he paused to look out the window, one of the blades, or two of them, was instantly at work. It might be that only a few seconds could be put on

128

the task, but each stroke was a scratch towards success.

Files made of diamond chips could not have eaten into the tough steel of the bars more quickly than the chilled steel-toothed blades, but even so there were four cuts to make, and it was not until the day before their appointed hour of execution that they could feel any assured hope. Probably they could saw through the bars the rest of the way that night. At any rate it was time to send out the warning. So on the bottom of his tin plate after lunch that day, with the point of a blade, Jack Sherry inscribed a cross. Inside the plate he put another, then the two could sit close to the bars and, during the rest of the day, work with the saw blades while they carried on the pretense of their card game.

At supper time came their answer. At the side of each deep tin dish there was inscribed a hieroglyph consisting of an involved scroll. Sherry had told Garvin what to look for in the way of a symbol. They looked at one another now with something more than a smile.

"Myers is up to his promise," said Sherry. "By morning we'll be free."

"Don't say it!" protested Bill Garvin. "If you count the chickens before they're hatched, you'll have the luck against you."

His pallor and the tremor of his hands made Sherry look suddenly down in terror. He had known that the death house days had worn down his partner, but he had not dreamed that the soul of Bill Garvin had been rubbed as thin as this.

Mickey Duveen was on guard that night. He chose to stand at the bars of the cell for two hours, from midnight on, telling just how long it took a hanged man to die.

"I've seen 'em for twenty minutes with the doctor listening before the heart stopped. Long as the heart keeps workin', there you are, chokin', stranglin', dyin', wishin' to be dead, and have

129

it over with," said Mickey Duveen.

They gave him no answer. Bill Garvin pretended to be snoring at last, and Duveen cursed them and went away.

They were at the bars in a moment. The days of rest and good food in the death house had given to Sherry the greater part of his lost strength. He used it now to wrench at the partially cut bars until one of them came away suddenly and, with the jerk, set the length of the bar humming softly. He put both hands on the second bar and pulled. It broke above silently enough, but the lower shred of remaining steel snapped loudly. A faint groan from Bill Garvin was the echo to that noise. Almost instantly there was a hurrying footfall up the corridor. "We're done for! We're as good as hanging by the neck, right now," said Garvin.

Mickey Duveen appeared. "What in hell's happening?" he barked.

Sherry stood just opposite the gap in the bars, pressing close to them so that the missing portions might be less noticeable.

"I want to hear some more about what happens," said Sherry. "After they put the black cap over my face, what happens then?"

"You'd like to know, eh? You think you'd be able to get ready for it, do you? You think you'd steel yourself?" sneered Mickey Duveen. "By the way you ask, I know that you're gonna be a damn' sniveling cur when the time comes to. . . ."

He had stepped a little closer to drive home his prophecy. Now the hand, the arm, the whole shoulder and side of Sherry thrust through the gap. His fingers clutched the thick throat of Mickey and dragged the guard with a slam against the steel rods. Mickey Duveen, the protest and the groan throttled in his throat, sank limply to the floor. He had managed to draw a gun but that was all.

Now Sherry stepped out, the first stride towards freedom. Garvin was instantly after him. Mickey Duveen, still senseless, they bound and gagged, and Duveen's second gun went into the hands of Garvin before Sherry picked the guard up and thrust him through the bars into the vacant cell.

"We ought to tap him over the head," muttered Garvin.

"We did no senseless murder to get in here. We'll do no senseless murder to get out," answered Sherry. "Have you got the keys?"

The hands of Bill Garvin were trembling so that he could hardly try the keys in the lock of the big steel door at the end of the corridor. Sherry had to make the attempt, and it succeeded almost at once. The massive door, on its well-oiled hinges, sighed open before them. Before their feet appeared a steep flight of stairs. Another door barred the way at the bottom.

When they reached it, the keys were used again until this barrier also had been penetrated. They stepped straight into the desolate spaciousness of the prison dining room. This they crossed, Sherry in the lead, revolving in his mind the plan of the prison that Jake Myers had furnished to him.

Beyond the dining room they passed into the prison yard, dwarfed in its dimensions by the towering height of the walls. On those walls figures moved, small, black against the stars. Those were the guards, rifles on shoulders. How could they be expected to pierce the shadows beneath them and see the skulking forms of the two big men who slipped along close to the prison building?

They came to the small postern door. A guard appeared before them, shadowy, swift. He whispered, as he turned the lock: "Get through . . . get fast . . . for God's sake move along!"

They moved along, willingly enough into the freer, sweeter air beyond. They had before them the long slope with the three little guard houses, each topped with a searchlight that could be made to revolve or play here and there. As the door of the postern jarred quietly shut behind them, a sound burst upon them, falling on their ears like towers of crashing brass. It sent a roaring echo up the slope. A booming note rose in answer from the prison yard inside. The two fugitives stood entranced with terror. Again the sound struck at them — it was the prison bell, rapidly hammering out the alarm.

They ran forward at full speed. It seemed that, if they could once pass the line of the guard houses, all would be well. But in those houses were instant responses, a rising to life. The searchlights cast startled, brilliant glances along the slope. From the prison, near the main gate, a rifle shot sounded. Instantly all the three long arms of the searchlights were extended to touch that spot. By the time they recoiled from that false alarm, Garvin and big Jack Sherry were beyond the line of the guard houses.

# VIII

## "JUMBO TAKES THE TRAIL"

They were first sighted north, near the town of Durant. A thousand men took rifles, mounted horses, and rode in pursuit. Out of that swarming wasps' nest they disappeared and were seen again trying to break through the western passes of the mountains, but the entire countryside rose up for the manhunt. The newspapers were carrying headlines every day. The prices on the heads of the two men were mounting. They doubled straight back east, mounted on two good stolen horses. The men of the town of Hoya chased the fugitives for three days and turned them south. And in all of these parts of the chase, two figures appeared constantly. One was Sheriff Champ Wallace and the other was that famous gunman, Jumbo Joe.

This was what had happened when at last two fugitives turned into Calder Basin on two lean, travel-weary horses. The basin was as hot and savage a bit of desert as either of them had ever seen, but they entered it with a certain relaxation of the mind. As Bill Garvin said: "They've stopped us on three sides. The fourth side is where all our luck has to be. Now we'll find it."

It was late in the afternoon before they gained the basin proper, a huge bowl of rock and sand that sloped down to little blue Calder Lake at the bottom. The only outlet of the lake was underground, but the water was always fresh and cool. To Sherry and Bill Garvin the lake was like a blue eye of heaven.

They made a long, long halt at this place. An entire two hours they spent — broiling rabbit, eating the meat they had grown to detest, and then re-saddling and mounting their horses. The two were sun blackened now from constant exposure. The whole of Jack Sherry's wasted strength had returned to him. Only in the face he was altered and would never be the same again. His voice was never lifted in song along the trail. The fine markings of pain made him seem years older. Riding shoulder-to-shoulder up the southern trail, the two exchanged quiet glances, now and then. Neither of them would have given up his place beside his comrade for all the gold of the world.

"What would you aim to do now?" asked Bill Garvin.

"Start far off, some place, and begin small, and save our coin, and then begin to build up a small herd."

"We'll never get far enough away to make a start. Not with a hanging waiting for us whenever we're caught up."

The truth of this weighed like lead on the mind of Sherry. They had climbed their horses through withering heat up the steep southern face of the basin, where the trail followed, rather too closely, the long, dangerous slope of a true devil's slide, a sleek mass of sand and rock rubble that looked ready to start pouring again at the least disturbance. Now, as they reached the jagged rocks above, Bill Garvin canted his head to one side and lifted his hand.

"Horses!"

"How many?" asked Sherry.

"Two."

"And there's two of us . . . so ride straight ahead and the best man lives," growled Sherry.

Garvin glanced across at his friend in amazement. "Have you started *hunting* for fights?" he demanded.

"I'm tired of sneaking out of the way of trouble."

"You're only a fool kid," declared Bill Garvin.

Sherry turned in the saddle and stared fiercely into Garvin's eyes with savage words forming on his lips, but instead of uttering them he merely smiled and drew his mustang back among the rocks. They were hardly out of view — the dust that their horses had raised was still visible in thin traces through the air — when two riders came into sight through the gap among the boulders. Sherry found himself looking at Sheriff Champ Wallace and big Jumbo Joe.

They came on eagerly, the tired, dusty horses beginning to press forward when they smelled the water in the distance. They had just passed Sherry's hiding place when he shouted: "Stick 'em up!"

Jumbo Joe cried out a curse. The sheriff silently thrust his hands slowly above his head. "It's no use, Jumbo," he said. "They don't miss at a range like this. Stick up your hands."

"After all this . . . ," groaned Jumbo, and his reluctant hands slowly thrust up.

"Fan 'em, Sherry," said Bill Garvin.

From each of them Sherry took a pair of guns as well as the Winchester which fitted down into a slanting saddle boot. There were no other weapons except two good hunting knives. The sheriff and Jumbo Joe, dismounted, were permitted to sit on a rock in the shadow of a great boulder. The sheriff was perfectly calm. Jumbo was the color of green jade, but he was calm also.

"It's a matter of knocking us in the head, I suppose?" asked Champ Wallace.

"Maybe not you," answered Garvin. "This here . . . this long-faced swine of a Jumbo Joe, he's gotta die. He should've died long ago. Wallace, whatever made you hook up with him?"

The sheriff answered: "When you ride to a fight, it's a hell of a lot the best way to take a fighting man along."

"Maybe so," said Garvin, "and take a crook to catch a crook. Is that the idea?"

Sherry said: "Jumbo, where'll you have it? Through the head or through the belly?"

Jumbo Joe said nothing. There was nothing human in his eyes.

"Give him a gun, Bill," said Sherry. "I won't murder him."

"Yeah. It has to be a fair fight," said Garvin. "But look at it this way . . . if Jumbo's wiped out, there's no way we'll ever get the real truth to be known."

"You think he'll talk?" sneered Sherry.

"Jumbo," said Garvin, "do you want to take your chance right now with the guns or will you tell the truth about During Gulch and the Overland and let the sheriff take you to jail?"

Big Jumbo looked at the gun which Garvin was ready to offer, and his eyes glittered. Then he looked at Sherry, standing tall, alert, hungry for the kill. "Well, why not take the fun as I find it?" asked Jumbo. "I'm ready to talk about During Gulch. Me and Walton done the job."

"You and Walton!" the sheriff said. "How come the crooked money in the hands of Sherry and Garvin then?"

"We bought some wet cattle off of them and paid 'em in the Overland cash."

"You dog!" growled the sheriff. He looked ready to smash his fist into the face of Jumbo, but he held his hand at the last

135

moment. "Then there's nothing on Bill Garvin? There's nothing on Sherry except the killing of a gent that the law already wanted?" he demanded. "Wait a minute. I got to figure this out."

"This'll help you. You'll think better with this." Garvin passed a Colt back to the sheriff. Champ Wallace looked down at the gun and up at big Jumbo Joe.

"I've got a mind to rob the hangman," he said. "No wonder you took the trail. No wonder you wouldn't rest quiet till Garvin and Sherry were dead. Wait a minute . . . Sherry, step back through the pass here, till you can see three gents riding to the east. They were heading for Blakeman's, thinking you might go that way. Take your coat off and try to wave them in, will you? This manhunt's ended."

Sherry, with a nod to Garvin, pulled off his jacket and went back through the rocks until he made out a dwindling dust cloud towards the east. A wild shout from the sheriff and the explosion of a gun made him whirl. He heard one thundering word from Jumbo Joe and then the ringing hoofs of a horse.

He could guess what had happened. The terrible hands of Jumbo could work miracles if they were not watched every instant. He knew this, as he leaped back to the place where he had left the trio. The sheriff was trying to get back to his feet after the blow that had felled him. Well down the trail Jumbo was fleeing on the best of the horses. Bill Garvin lay flat on his back with his arms thrown out, crosswise, and a streak of crimson across his forehead.

# IX

## "COURAGE SHOWDOWN"

He tried three snap shots at the fugitive, but his hand was crazy with jumping nerves, and Jumbo's howl of mockery drifted back at him. He flung himself on the nearest horse and rushed it down the trail, but in a moment he realized that he would never overtake Jumbo with such a mount. His bulk was close to that of Jumbo's, and he had an inferior animal beneath him.

He looked up with a groan that was a prayer. The sun-flooded sky seemed to tremble above him with his own wrath. Then deliberately he turned the horse from the trail and right onto the sheer face of the slide. Off to the side and below came the shout of Jumbo Joe. Sherry could see him shaking a fist above his head in a glory of joy. But a moment later Jumbo was riding for his life, while a shower of loosened rocks and sand went skipping about him, flung down by Sherry's own sliding horse.

The landslide increased. The whole face of the treacherous slope came alive. A great moving arm shot out, gathered up Jumbo Joe, and whirled him and his mustang into that fatal confusion. Sherry saw that and then the dust blinded him. In that blindness he found his horse veering, staggering down the slope. The first shock of the slide struck the waters of the lake with a crash that must have been audible for miles. Then something thudded against the head of Sherry, and his wits were gone. When he recovered them, he was lying flat, half buried in debris. The wind was tearing away the great cloud of dust.

But where was Jumbo Joe? He saw the giant now, a staggering shape through the whirling dust, busily pulling a Winchester from the side of his dead horse. Sherry started to drag himself to his feet. Then he knew suddenly that he was helpless to move. His right leg was broken above the knee. There was not much pain; there was chiefly a numbness. There was only one thing for him to do, and he did it. He grasped a jagged rock with his right hand and then lay back, inert, still, his eyes a trifle open, as the eyes of a dead man should be. He heard the fellow coming. He saw the shadow falling across him.

"Get up!" yelled Jumbo. "Get up and fight like a man, you sick rat! Or are you dead?" He kicked Sherry heavily. He leaned over. He actually plucked at the lids of Sherry's eyes and peered down into them. "Dead . . . they look dead enough," said Jumbo. "But I'll make sure!" He shifted his rifle.

With his left hand, Sherry caught at the gun. It exploded, driving a bullet into the ground close by his face. And with his right hand that grasped the rock Sherry struck for the nearest leg of the giant. He felt the shinbone crunch under the blow. Jumbo, with a howl, fell right across his breast, reaching for his throat.

That was it. Wild beasts strike for the jugular, and the grip of a fighting man should be for the same spot. He felt the grip of Jumbo crushing his neck. He was lost. He tried to press down his chin against the wrists of Jumbo and so weaken the hold, but it was like pressing against double bars of rough, unhammered iron. The effort only seemed to press the fingers of Jumbo deeper into his windpipe. Darkness covered his brain, shot through with red.

Then he remembered lying out in the wilderness with the bleeding wound in his body, waiting for death. At that time he had been close to dying, and yet he had endured. He would endure now. If he fought, without surrendering one scruple of his effort, no matter how he was being throttled . . . !

With regular pulsations, he drove his thumbs deeper and deeper through the rubbery muscles into the hollow of Jumbo's throat. But it was no use. He was dying. He had not a second to live, for his lungs would burst with fire. But then he saw in a glimpse through the blackness of his mind a horribly contorted face above him, the tongue thrusting out from frightfully writhing lips. The tongue had been bitten deep.

A fresh fury of strength came into the hands of Sherry at that. His grip suddenly redoubled, for hope was vaguely in him. At once, like an answer, the grasp of the giant left his neck. Huge fists beat wildly against his head, against his face. Vast hands grasped his wrists and tried to tear his clutch loose. But his own hands were riveted to his work. In another instant the swelling power of the flesh he was strangling gave way, the weight of Jumbo fell loosely across his breast, and lay there . . . still.

They got Sherry back to Travis Junction in a horse litter. The Careys sent the litter and the horses for it, and they came themselves to oversee the procedure. On the way back Paula Carey walked on one side of the litter and Bill Garvin, a bandage around his wounded head, walked on the other.

They put Sherry in bed with a weight pulling on his right leg after the doctor had set it. He lay pale, sleeping so profoundly that Paula, on one side of the bed, ventured to say: "All right, Bill. We won't need you now. You get a rest. I'll take care of him."

"You'll take care of him?" muttered Bill Garvin. "How the hell should I . . . I mean, what the devil . . . ?"

"What right have I?" asked the girl.

"Yeah? Well, what I mean to say . . . ," began Bill Garvin, "it would be a hell of a note if he woke up and didn't find me, now wouldn't it? Besides what right have you horning in?"

"As soon as he wakes up, I'm going to ask him to let me have a right."

Garvin stared helplessly at her. "Oh," he said, "that's the way of it, eh? You're gonna try to steal him, are you?"

"No," she answered, "I could never do that. But I might share him."

Garvin sighed. "It says in the book," he quoted, "that women are the root of all evil."

Max Brand wrote a total of five short novels about Bull Hunter, that gentle giant of a man who sees so deeply into the human soul. "Bullets with Sense" was the first, appearing in Street & Smith's *Western Story Magazine* in the issue dated 7/9/21. This was later combined with the second, "Bull Hunter Feels His Oats" in *Western Story Magazine* (8/13/21), to form the book-length novel, BULL HUNTER (Chelsea House, 1924), published under the byline David Manning (even though the stories appeared under the Max Brand byline in the magazine). In 1981 Dodd, Mead & Company reprinted BULL HUNTER, this time under the Max Brand byline, and it is now available in a paperback edition from Leisure Books. In the first two short novels, Bull Hunter is intent on tracking down the notorious gunfighter, Pete Reeve, only for the two to end up becoming partners. In "Outlaws All," the third short novel to feature Bull Hunter and contained in OUTLAWS ALL: A WESTERN TRIO (Five Star Westerns, 1996), Bull manages to tame the wolf dog known as The Ghost. At the conclusion of that story, Pete Reeve expresses his belief that this combination of the two partners with Diablo, the stallion, and The Ghost, " 'can snap our fingers at the world, even if the world makes outlaws of us all.' " "The Wolf Strain," appearing originally in *Western Story Magazine* (9/24/21), continues their story.

# THE WOLF STRAIN
## A Bull Hunter Story

# I

## "BEFORE THE CAMP FIRE"

The camp fire had changed from bright to dull gold and, finally, being chiefly a wisp of smoke and a bed of dying embers, it threw only enough light to pick out the forms near it in flat, black shadows. The faces of the two men were indistinguishable, but their silhouettes were strongly contrasted. One was a wide-shouldered monster, and the other was as remarkably meager as his companion was large. He sat with slumping shoulders like an adolescent child.

"Look at 'em," said the little man. "Look at The Ghost working at the cur, Bull."

The big man leaned and stirred the embers. By the red glow which sprang up in answer, it was possible to see a mighty hand, not made to take and to hold but to seize and crush. His voice in answer to the question, however, was a smooth, gentle bass.

"I been watching, Pete, all day, and I been wishing that Dunkin would come back and look after his dog."

"Look after him?" asked Pete. "Why, it looks to me like the dog could take care of himself. The Ghost is fair busting himself to make friends."

"I dunno," sighed Bull. "I dunno." And he shook his big head.

In the meantime they continued to observe the two dogs. There was as great a contrast between the animals as between the men.

The Ghost was the huge, gray-coated fellow. He could only be called a dog by courtesy, for he had the big shoulders and the wise head of the loafer wolf. If he were observed running the hills alone, any man in the mountains would reach for his rifle and try a shot without questioning the identity of his target. Yet, in spite of appearances, The Ghost was nonetheless a dog, for no loafer wolf since the beginning of time had ever become tame. He was not only peaceably stretched beside a camp fire with two men, but he was doing his best to make friendly advances to a mongrel cur that lay within the circle of the fire's warmth.

It was an important time in the life of the huge wolf-like dog. Many weeks before he had roamed the mountains like a true wolf and a dreaded one. A long pursuit by men and packs of hounds had driven him, wounded and close to his last fight, into the cabin of Bull Hunter. There he had found a rescuer, a healer of his wounds, a master, and finally a friend. The dog blood in The Ghost, as he was known throughout the mountains on account of his pale gray coat and his fearful depredations among the cattle, had come to the surface, and the wolf in him had been steadily diminishing. But not until today had he made a definite avowal of his change of caste. He was attempting to make friends with the big, fierce mongrel on the ground by the fire.

His methods were not altogether competent to inspire friendly confidence. They began when, after a long survey of the mongrel, he rose from his place beside Bull Hunter and began to stalk around the other dog in a wide circle, moving with stiff-jointed steps that showed he would be instantly ready to fight if the occasion demanded. The mongrel flattened his head to the earth and watched the progress of the gray giant with rolling eyes. He bared his teeth, but he had not the courage to growl. A growl would be a challenge, but the bared teeth merely showed that, while he invited no trouble, he would fight to the last ditch if the pinch came. In the meantime he gathered his hind feet well under him, every muscle of his legs quivering and ready to send him off in a flying leap, should The Ghost stop his promenade and attack. But The Ghost made no offer to fight. He continued to move solemnly about the other, viewing him from every angle. Finally he went straight up to the other and, standing not a yard away, pricked his ears and slowly wagged his tail. The mongrel twitched his own tail, but it was a perfunctory response.

To make his meaning clear, The Ghost turned and marched about the camp fire in a swift circle, a ghostly figure in the night. Plainly he was inviting the other to come with him for a romp across the hills, for he looked back as he ran. The mongrel shuddered and pressed his body closer to the warmed earth. *Follow that slayer into the darkness?* he seemed to ask.

The Ghost returned and now stood with his head cocked to one side, regarding the other with a wistful curiosity. There was a certain pathos in his attitude, as though he were striving mightily to learn the language of this fellow and finding it impossible. At last his impatience found vent in a deep-throated growl. His antics had been all dog, but his growl was all wolf.

"I think maybe you're right," said Pete Reeve to his companion, hearing the snarl of The Ghost. "In five minutes they'll either be friends or fighting. Dunkin may come back and find himself minus a dog." He chuckled again. "And that'd sure make him mad. He loves that dog."

"He won't be minus a dog," answered Bull Hunter.

"How come?" asked the little man. "You don't think the cur yonder would have a fighting chance against The Ghost?"

"The Ghost would kill him in five seconds," said Bull soberly, "but I promised Dunkin, when he left, that I would keep The Ghost away from his dog. So I must."

"I remember," said Pete Reeve. "When Dunkin left, he swore

you'd have to account to him if anything went wrong with his dog." He broke off and laughed softly. "Dunkin is a pretty hard sort but, if he knew you better, he'd have sooner bitten his tongue than talked so big to you, Bull."

Bull Hunter waved this implied compliment away. "Where has Dunkin gone?" he asked.

The little man jerked his head to one side and looked intently at his companion. "Ain't you guessed?" he asked sharply.

Bull Hunter shook his head.

"Well," said Reeve in the same sullen manner, "I ain't handing out any information. Besides, I don't altogether know. I ain't riding with Dunkin tonight."

"I think I can guess," said Bull Hunter sadly.

"Guess all you want to," replied the other.

An unreasonable irritation seemed to seize him. He rose and paced up and down with quick small steps until he had mastered his outburst of temper. Then he came back, rested his hand for a single instant on the muscular shoulder of his friend, and sat down again in his former place. Bull Hunter had replied to this silent apology with a nod of his head, but he continued to stare thoughtfully at the fire.

Pete Reeve was a definitely outlawed man, accused of many violent crimes, and here was Bull Hunter, a law-abiding man, sitting at the side of one with a price on his head. But the outlaw was also his best friend. Hunter had made one great effort to keep his friend within the law. When that effort failed, he had first helped Pete to dodge his pursuers and then ridden with him into the mountain desert. Now he was in a quandary. Peter Reeve, riding where he willed and never long in one place, lived on the spoils of society. Bull Hunter, living as an honest man, could only exist on the charity of Pete so long as he rode with him. He detested this life of dependence. Yet he could not persuade himself to leave his friend. He was a restraining influence, keeping Pete from running amuck, as the terrible little gunfighter was apt to do at any time when the temptation became strong enough.

Now by the camp fire Bull was full of doubts. Dunkin, who had joined them a few days before and had ridden off that morning, was an old acquaintance of Pete's. Dunkin was on the face of him a bad one. Bull had from the first moment hated the swagger of the fellow, and his thin-lipped, twisting smile, and his malicious eye. He had not the slightest doubt that Dunkin had left their temporary camp to ride off on some errand of mischief. And Bull, writhing at the thought, felt that his crime would be the greater of the two, if he accepted the hospitality of the other. But what should he do? Could he leave Pete Reeve a hopeless victim to the evil influence of the depraved Dunkin?

It seemed that Reeve's mind had been running in the same direction, for now he said: "Men are like dogs, Bull. I'm like The Ghost, except that he's big for his kind and I'm little for mine. The Ghost has run wild all his life and raised the devil. So have I. The Ghost found a friend in you, and now he's trying to turn decent and be civilized. I found a friend in you, too, Bull, and I'm doing the same things as The Ghost. I'm trying to get civilized and live decent. But I don't think The Ghost will stay tame . . . he'll turn wild again, and so will I." He sighed and shook his head. "And in the end, we'll both have to leave you, Bull."

"In the end," said Bull, smiling sadly, "I'll have to follow you." He turned his head sharply. "Steady!"

The Ghost obeyed the command by springing six feet backward. He stood with head lowered, a snaky, formidable, cunning head, seen thus in profile. The mongrel twitched himself about and faced the gray giant in the new position.

"You see," said Pete Reeve, "that The Ghost can't make friends with the cur, and so he wants to fight him. If you won't let

147

him fight, you and him will have trouble. And then he'll leave. A wild dog ain't never going to be really happy with a tame master. And a man with a wolf strain is just the same way."

In one respect at least he had spoken the truth. His voice was hardly quiet when The Ghost, having tried in vain all manner of friendly advances toward the dog and having been repelled with terror and disgust at each attempt, gathered himself and flung straight at the mongrel. The latter stood up with a brief howl of terror, wavered for the split part of a second between a desire to run and a knowledge that he would be overtaken instantly if he fled, and then bared his teeth to meet that attack as well as he might.

The Ghost was not one of those who strive to win battles by sheer bulk and brawn, regardless of the punishment they receive. He was one of those terrible and wary fighters who slash another to pieces without receiving much punishment in return. Now, though he came like a driving arrow at the mongrel, he intended no battering assault. He swerved and, shooting past the other, slashed him down the shoulder as he shot by. Then he whirled at a little distance for another charge. The mongrel was himself an old and practiced fighter. Against an ordinary wolf he would have put up a fair battle, but he was unable to cope with this whirlwind of muscle and teeth. He turned to meet the new attack, but he turned too late and would have received the great teeth of The Ghost in his throat had not a rescuer intervened. Bull Hunter lunged up and across the fire, a mighty figure. His two outstretched hands caught the breast and throat of The Ghost, as the wolf dog sprang. Despite his weight the shock staggered him. For a moment they stood, a strange pair of combatants, the wolf dog forced erect on his hind legs and almost as huge as the man.

The battle lust was hot in The Ghost. He had forgotten that it was his master who checked him. He only knew that this was

148

a bar which kept him from getting at the mongrel again. All his primitive killing instincts were aroused. Twice, swinging his head from side to side, his teeth clashed as loudly as the closing of a steel trap as he strove to get at the arms of the man. Before he could bite again, he was lifted high up and cast crashing down to the ground.

The force of the fall stunned him. When he gained his feet, he stood trembling on his braced legs and growling feebly at his master. Then, his brain partially clearing, he backed slowly away, slinking closer and closer to the ground. Bull Hunter followed him carefully, his hand extended, his voice softened almost to pleading.

"Steady, boy. Couldn't let you kill. Steady, old boy!"

"He's gone, Bull," said Pete Reeve with a sort of cruel satisfaction. "There's all our work undone by one taste of flesh." He broke into shrill, mirthless laughter. It had been a horrible thing to see, that battle of the man and the wolf and, having been greatly moved, Pete laughed. For it was his nature to go by opposites.

Laughter was the one thing which the wolf dog dreaded the most. This was the one attribute which no other animal had. This was the thing which The Ghost trembled at and shrank from. He had loved Bull Hunter because the big man rarely laughed. There was no mockery in his nature. But now the laughter of Pete Reeve came to The Ghost as the final blow. He had been beaten and crushed by the physical strength of a man, and now the sense of man's superiority was borne to him in derisive mockery. He turned upon Pete Reeve with a snarl so terrible that the little man instinctively reached for his gun. The Ghost wheeled and faded instantly into the friendly night. That was his country; firelight was the country of man.

# II

## "THE LOCKET"

Filled with dread, Bull Hunter first followed at a quick walk then broke into a run, shouting after the fugitive. Presently he saw a faintly outlined form glimmer on the top of a hill and dip away on the other side. He knew that The Ghost, whose confidence he had won with such pain and trouble, whom he had come to love as if he were a human friend, was indeed gone and had fled back to his own kind.

Bull came back to the camp fire, stumbling like a stunned man. Pete Reeve, in the darkness, failed to note the emotion of his friend. He broke into fresh laughter.

"He ran like a whipped cur, Bull. He's gone back to his cattle killing. I think it was more my laughing than your throwing him down that drove him off."

His fresh peals of mirth fell away to silence when the deep, stern voice of Bull Hunter cut in on him. "Yep, it was your laughing that done it. Otherwise I'd've won him back. It was your laughing and your friend's cur dog."

The face of Pete Reeve wrinkled with pain and flushed with anger, but he controlled himself instantly. If he were a little inclined to mock the big, slow-moving, slow-thinking fellow in ordinary times, on occasions when Bull Hunter became grave, Pete Reeve instantly showed his respect. He held out his hand now.

"I'm sorry, Bull," he said. "Come to think of it, that was a fool thing I done, laughing at The Ghost when he was kind of on edge that way."

Bull Hunter accepted both the hand and the apology. It was impossible for him to hold malice for more than a moment. When he sat down again by the fire, he was buried in deep and gloomy thought. It was no light thing to him, this loss of the wolf dog who had been companion to him for so many days. In his imagination he saw again the shaggy, wounded form that had crept into his cabin and cowered in the corner, hopeless and weak but ready to fight his pursuers to the last ditch. And he traced swiftly the progress of his influence over The Ghost until the wolf dog had come to obey not only his voice but even his gestures and the very glances of his eyes. Now, all in a moment, the wild nature of the beast had flared up, and he was gone back to his kind.

The neigh of a horse far off, a tired horse returning to its home, broke in on his thoughts. Presently he could make out a horseman climbing the hillside below them. Pete Reeve was already on his feet, gathering wood to freshen the fire.

"It's Dunkin," he said, "and he's come back lucky if he's come back this early."

This mention of luck brought a gloomy look from Bull Hunter, but the little man went on about his work, oblivious of his partner. Presently Dunkin came out of the night and dismounted into the lights of the newly leaping flames of the camp fire, a lithe, long fellow with a sinister face. He was gaily clad for a desert rider, with all the cowpuncher's finery of spurs and boots and silk shirt and big bandanna, Mexican style. But the dust of long riding had reduced his flaring colors to a common drab. He greeted his companions with no word but drew a small sack from one of his saddle bags and flung it with a melodious clinking down on the ground by the fire.

"There it is," he said.

Bull Hunter dropped his head, but Pete Reeve picked up the sack and weighed it with a brightening face. "All good stuff, Dunkin, eh?"

"Good stuff? Would I take it if it wasn't?"

Pete untied the mouth of the sack and peered inside. "Come, take a look, Bull," he called cheerily. But the big man shook his head.

"Sulking again, eh?" asked Dunkin, eyeing Bull. "Well, maybe you'll grow up one of these days, Hunter."

"Maybe," said Bull.

"I wished I'd been along with you, Dunkin," said the little man, and his bright, nervous eyes roamed over the face of Dunkin, as though he were striving to read in the features of his companion the story of what had happened that day.

"I'd rather have you along on a party than any gent that ever wore spurs," said Dunkin flatteringly, "but you wouldn't be no help down yonder in that territory." He waved toward the lowlands. "If talk gets dull for me when I'm down yonder, I just mention your name, Pete, and then they buzz around like a lot of hornets. Old Culver come in and raised the price on you by fifteen hundred, and that's started a new posse on your trail."

"Know which way?"

"Just exactly the wrong way," said Dunkin. "They sure don't dream you're up here."

"Maybe I'll give 'em to know where I am before I'm through," said Pete darkly. "Maybe I'll get tired of having them put up money for me, like I was a hoss that'd run away, or something like that. Maybe I'll show 'em how many men they'll need to have if they ever do run me down, which they won't! But" —and he ended with a sigh after his boasting— "it's hard to be a marked man. You'll know when they get onto you, Dunkin."

"When they get onto me! But they ain't never going to," said Dunkin, "because I keep a free hand. I don't tie myself down with a lot of dead weight. I travel light."

He indicated Bull Hunter with a jerk of his thumb. The big man did not see, but he understood the meaning of the words without having seen the gesture that accompanied them. He knew that for a week Dunkin had been trying to make Pete Reeve leave his sluggish companion and strike out on the free, swift trail of the lawless with him as a partner. Sooner or later he feared that Pete would sink under the temptation. In the meantime, while Pete cooked for the newcomer, the latter sat down on his heels to smoke a cigarette and tell of the adventure.

"It was easy. I just sort of happened to be walking down the road when the old boy drove along in his buckboard. He stopped to chin, just the way I knew he would. First thing off he seen the saddle marks on my trousers. But I started telling him a cock-and-bull story about losing my hoss, and pretty soon I got up close and shoved my gat under his nose. He's a fast one on the draw, but he didn't have no chance that way. I had him cold. Well, I went through him and got his guns, and the old cuss had two of 'em. Then I grabbed the bag. Payroll for this month, I figure, and a stake that'll float us for a pretty long time.

"When he seen me with the bag in my hand, he loosened up and began to get fresh. So for that I went through him again and got his own wallet with fifty in it and a locket that was strung around his neck. He went plumb nutty when I got that and told me I'd burn in hell for taking his daughter's picture off'n him. But who's been cutting up my dog?"

The last was a veritable yell of astonishment and rage, as the mongrel, with his wounded shoulder, crawled to the feet of his master. Luckily for him The Ghost had slipped a little in his spring, and his snap, as he got past, had been a fraction of an inch short of his intention. Therefore the wound was a shallow gash which would heal quickly. In the meantime the crimson scab made it seem like a death wound.

"The Ghost," said Pete Reeve.

"That murdering wolf of yours!" exclaimed Dunkin, trembling with anger, and he stalked over toward the big man. Size meant nothing in a gunfight, and Dunkin was a fighter with guns and guns only. The bulk of Bull Hunter made him only an easier target. Dunkin was fearless. He hated the quiet honesty of the big man; he hated him because it was Bull who kept Pete Reeve from running amuck on the long trail. Now all his hatred came trembling in his voice.

"You can say good bye to that dirty wolf," he declared, "and you can say it *pronto*. Where is he?"

"Cleaned out," said Pete Reeve, watching the two in growing anxiety. He saw Bull Hunter raise his head for the first time and, though he made no reply to Dunkin, Hunter watched the face of the man with a strange steadiness that foreboded no good. "He cleaned out, Dunkin, and it was Bull who saved the hide of your dog. He took The Ghost by the throat and banged him to the ground."

It may have been the words of Pete — it may have been the quiet, straight-looking eyes of Hunter that cooled the ire of Dunkin — but his tone changed at once. "Took The Ghost by the throat with his bare hands . . . that dirty wolf?" asked Dunkin. He retreated a step, watching Bull Hunter with a new respect.

"That was what he done," said Pete dryly. "Here's your chuck, ready. Come on and eat. Besides, on account of your dog, Bull lost The Ghost, and he was sure fond of him."

"That's a pile different," admitted Dunkin. "Makes me kind of sorry I busted out like I just done." He fumbled in his pocket, and then he drew out a chain and locket. "Here's that picture I pinched. Maybe you'd like to see it. Ain't it a hummer?"

Bull extended his hand and took the trinket. Awkwardly he snapped the locket open. It was a beautiful subject, beautifully done. A miniaturist of no mean ability, wandering through the West to regain his health, had painted it, and he had done justice to his sitter. With an exclamation of delight Bull Hunter received the trinket reverently in both his opened hands.

"Hit the flint that time and drew a spark, I reckon," said Dunkin, stepping back. "Bull's all wrought up, Pete."

The little man rose and went to his big friend and looked over the shoulder of Bull at the painting. It was a beautiful, dark-eyed girl, and the play of the firelight gave a peculiar illusion of life to her smile.

"It's her," said Bull Hunter at last. "It's Mary Hood, Pete."

He closed the locket suddenly and stared at Dunkin as though he were angry that the eyes of the man had rested on even the representation of that face. He asked coldly: "You took it off'n her father, you say?"

"Sure, son."

"You robbed him of it maybe?" went on Bull.

Dunkin saw the new drift at once and met it willingly. "If you don't like it because it was grabbed, give it back to me at once."

"It's got to go back to her," said Bull gravely, "and your hands will never touch it again."

Dunkin choked and then cursed explosively. "Go back to her? Not in a million years. Give that back to me, Hunter. You hear me talk?"

Pete Reeve drew back and watched quietly. He seemed to be judging the two men.

"Not in a million years . . . I won't give it back to you," said Bull, rising to his feet. "They ain't a man here that's good enough to carry her picture around. This is more'n most pictures. It's so like her it's almost as if there was part of her in it. And not one of us here is good enough to carry this around. It's going back. Mind that, Dunkin."

"Now, by . . . ," began Dunkin.

Pete Reeve intervened decisively, walking between the two men as if they had not been on the verge of a gun play. "You listen to me, Dunkin." And he took the arm of Dunkin and turned him away.

"I'll finish talking to you later," said Dunkin, looking at Hunter and going off with the little man.

"Now," said Pete Reeve softly, when they were well out of earshot. The dwindling camp fire had grown star-like behind them, even at that short distance. "I'll tell you that you was close to a bad bust, partner."

"Because of him?" asked Dunkin. "Say, Pete, them big ones are too slow, a lot too slow."

"I've seen him fight," said Pete with conviction, "and he can shoot. I taught him how."

Dunkin had been prepared for protest, but the last words made him close his mouth with a slight intake of breath that was almost a gasp. The speed and accuracy of Pete Reeve with a gun were grimly known facts in the mountain desert.

"There ain't any fear in him," said Pete. "He's gentle as a kid."

"Stupid gentle."

"Maybe you'd call it that. He's got more brains than anyone I ever seen, but he's queer, different from us. And he's too humble. He thinks slow, but he thinks sure, and he always comes out right. But don't make no mistake. He's the worst man to tangle with that you ever seen."

"I ain't taking nothing from nobody," said Dunkin with a sort of defensive ferocity.

"You don't have to. He won't ever mention it again, if you don't bring it up. And he won't bother you none."

"I don't think he will," said Dunkin. "Look back there! If he ain't rolling up in his blankets!"

"That's his way," replied Pete Reeve. "When most of us want to do a thing, we start right off, but Bull Hunter sleeps on it first, and then he starts to do it. But the point is that it always gets done. In the morning he'll start, and he'll get there. He

156

loves that girl, Dunkin. He seen her and loved her, but he got in a fight with her father, the same gent you stuck up today. You know Jack Hood is fast with a gun. But he was like a gent in a dream compared with Bull. Bull shot him down and hurt him pretty bad. Then he got away from the whole Dunbar outfit, including big Hal Dunbar himself, with me helping a little."

"Oh," said Dunkin. "You were there." He spoke as if the whole mystery were explained by Reeve's presence.

"Of course," went on Pete, "after shooting the girl's father, he couldn't very well stay around and make love to the girl, could he? Besides, he doesn't think he's good enough to have her wipe her shoes on him. So he's stayed away and ate his heart out, not even talking about her to me. Now here's the point of all this. Bull won't leave me, and he won't let me leave him, because he's afraid I'll start wrong ag'in. And me going near crazy for lack of something to do. Well, in the morning he'll try to get me to ride with him to the Dunbar ranch to see Mary Hood. But you and me will slip away before morning, and I'll leave him a note, saying we got a plan to work out, while he's riding up to the Dunbar ranch. Is that clear?"

"Clearest thing I ever heard," rejoined Dunkin joyously. "Pete, you and me working together can make a million. I always thought so!"

# III

## "BULL RIDES DIABLO"

So it happened that Bull Hunter, waking and standing up from his blankets in the first light of the morning, found not a sign of Reeve or Dunkin or the dog. Only the great black stallion,

Diablo, lifted his head from the place where he was cropping the dried grasses and whinnied a ringing good morning to his master. Aside from Diablo there was no living creature. The Ghost was gone. Dunkin was gone. And his best friend, his tried companion, Pete Reeve, had vanished like the wind. There was only Diablo and the mountains in the lonely morning light.

He found a note pinned to the bottom of his blankets:

Dear Bull:

Me and Dunkin have a little trip ahead. I know you ain't very happy about that sort of a trip, and I figured if you knew we was leaving, you'd come along just to take care of me, even if you had business of your own on hand. But I know that you're all set on going to the Dunbar ranch to see Mary Hood. And I sure don't blame you. Go and see her, and look sharp. Because Hal Dunbar and Jack Hood would both give a year of life to get a shot at you. I'll come back and find you later on. Good luck.

But, no matter how the letter was phrased, Bull felt that it was a case of desertion, plain and simple. Two great blows had fallen, one after the other. The Ghost was gone, and now Pete Reeve had followed, all in the space of a single night.

As if Diablo knew the heavy heart of the master, he came in a swinging gallop up the hill, circled the dead ashes of the camp fire thrice, and then plunged to a halt before Bull Hunter, a magnificent creature, close to seventeen hands. If Diablo were a mustang, then certainly he was a freakish throwback to the Barb type from which the horses of the Western plains and mountains developed. But no Barb had ever stood such a type. Perhaps a strain of the Thoroughbred had crossed the mustang blood. Whatever the reason Diablo was a glorious picture of a horse.

The quarters of an ordinary animal would have sunk beneath the huge burden of Bull Hunter in half an hour's travel. Even the mighty-muscled Diablo seemed small beside him, yet the black could carry that weight all day.

Now, with his bright eyes gleaming and his forelock blowing in the wind, he seemed to invite the master to gallop with him over the hills. The heart of Bull Hunter lightened a little. He passed a gentle hand over the proud curve of that neck and murmured a word or two in that kind voice that horses love to hear. Then a pool of water in the next hollow, rosy with the morning light, caught his eye. He threw himself on Diablo's back and passed at a wild gallop, careening among the rocks, to the edge of the water. Here he threw off his clothes and plunged in. The water, fresh from the snows and with the chill of them still in it, boiled around his shoulders. Why any living creature should seek a bath in water at that temperature, the very thought of which made the fetlock joints of Diablo ache, was beyond his imagining. But, since all the acts of the master were done for a reason and were generally good, the stallion came to the edge of the water, while the master swam with long-reaching overhand strokes, and tried the liquid with a tentative hoof. Diablo withdrew the wet hoof and shook it. Thereafter he kept to one side but, when Bull Hunter came out of the water, panting from the exercise and with the smile that tells of big muscles that have worked smoothly, Diablo stood near again and sniffed at the dripping skin. Bull Hunter swept off some of the water with his hands and rubbed away the rest with the rag that served him for a towel. When he had dressed, he leaped on the back of Diablo and rode singing back to his camp.

Not that all grief for the loss of The Ghost and Reeve was gone, but it was pushed to the back of his brain, just as the morning had pushed away the night from the peak and left huddling piles of blue-purple shadow in the gullies. For Bull was young, yes, very young; his pulses leaped easily. Being young, moreover, one thing could fill his mind. That one thing was Diablo. The stallion, at least, had not deserted him. As he felt the glorious strength of his body that swayed and trembled beneath him, a warmth of humble gratitude filled the heart of the giant. A child had taught him how to ride and control the stallion and, with the simple faith of a child, he still possessed Diablo. There was no battle between them, nothing of the conqueror and the conquered but a mutual confidence. That silent force, which had brought the wild wolf to the feet of big Hunter, had won Diablo also. In the beginning and in the end it was love. Not that the giant really understood this consciously. He could not analyze; he could only dream. He could not coldly and collectedly plan; he could only hope. In this very simplicity, perhaps, lay the strength of Bull Hunter, the thing that had helped him to do great and strange things in the mountain desert and that would help him to greater and stranger things before his death, until he became a legend and an inspiration to the strong men of the frontier. One of those characters, no matter how roughly, who help other men to lead clean lives.

He dared not stay long in the camp, for fear that he would begin to brood over the memory of the two whom he had lost. First he cooked a quick breakfast and noted with a pang that Pete Reeve had purposely left behind the choicest and best of their provisions. He found, too, tucked into his saddle bag a fat money belt with a comfortable supply of coin. It warmed his heart. It also made him wince with the realization that all these days he had really been so dependent upon the little gunfighter.

Breakfast over, he made his pack, strapped it behind the saddle, and was off across the hills on Diablo. Two shadows rose repeatedly, a gray wolf running before him and coming back to leap up at the nose of Diablo in playful ferocity, and a little

160

withered man with wise eyes who had once ridden beside him. But Bull Hunter drove the memories away by main force and allowed himself to see only one thing, the noble head and the shining neck of Diablo. He allowed himself to dream but one dream, that he was to see Mary Hood.

How he should again gain that great objective was beyond him. She was the daughter of the foreman of the greatest ranch in the mountains, the ranch owned by Hal Dunbar. The foreman he had shot down. Hal Dunbar he had foiled in a first effort to obtain Diablo. Besides, Hal Dunbar was expected to marry Mary Hood. Indeed, all things conspired to make the wished-for interview difficult. Dunbar, Hood, or any of their men, he well knew, would shoot him on sight without question and make their explanation later. But Bull Hunter let ways and means take care of themselves. His first task was to get to the Dunbar ranch.

It lay south, far south, over difficult ridges, a country steadily rougher and more beautiful. Three days went into that long ride. Some of the fat came off the sides of the stallion, so that, when the saddle was taken from him that night, Bull Hunter could see every muscle of the shoulder and hip, could have picked them out with thumb and forefinger almost. But he was not worried. He merely knew that Diablo was being trained down to racing condition.

In the rose of the dawn of the third morning he crossed the last range and came in sight of the big domain of the Dunbars. It was, indeed, a kingdom by itself, fenced with mountains in all directions and lying on a pleasantly rolling plateau.

There was fine tillable soil in that sweep of country. A little was already under the plow. A thousand times as much could be put to close cultivation, when a cleverer owner took the reins. Yet in a way it was better that there should be no such thrifty control. It left the fields wide and open, with only random fences, thousands and thousands of acres, spotted with single trees and lofty groves and cut with pleasant water courses and tumbled in places with long lines of natural hedges. Hal Dunbar, sitting his horse atop the crest of the range, could see it all. He could see the great grove of trees near the center of the domain, marking the house of the owner. He could even make out myriad small dots in the nearer pastures. Those were the grazing cattle. The wind changed and blew far off musical sounds to him, their lowing.

Such was the kingdom of the Dunbars. Bull Hunter was filled with a kind of sad happiness, knowing that Mary Hood was one day to be queen of it. If there was a sadness about his worship for her, it was only that she was removed to a great distance from him. She was to him like a masterpiece to a connoisseur, a dream of reality rather than an image of what had once been real.

It was dangerous work for Bull Hunter of all men to approach the ranch building in broad daylight, but he was not thinking of danger. He was feeling his nearness to the girl and, worst of all, he was coming up toward the rear of the house in which direction the barns and stables and corrals stretched. On this side also was the long bunkhouse, sure to be filled with men who had not yet ridden out to work, and all of the Dunbar men were sure to be hard riders and good marksmen. They were led by the redoubtable Jack Hood and by the yet more celebrated Hal Dunbar. But Bull Hunter rode in a dream.

He came out of the dream and the forest at the same time, and he saw before him first the corrals then the ranging stables and the bunkhouse and, beyond, set off with great terraced lawns and gardens, the house of Dunbar itself. The sight shocked him. He felt for the first time keenly the temerity of any single man daring to brave all this power. A moment later his abstract alarm was given a point.

A rider swung out from behind the nearest shed, saw the big

stranger, shouted once in shrill alarm, and then whipped his horse about and spurred out of sight, still shouting and crouched over the saddle horn, as though he feared a bullet might follow him. His fear was so real, Bull Hunter instinctively reached to the butt of his Colt.

# IV

## "THE CHASE"

In a moment his smile went out. The fellow had ridden in fear of his life and, now that Bull Hunter reflected, he remembered him to be Riley, the right-hand lieutenant of Hal Dunbar, particularly in all acts of deviltry. Riley had fled for fear of death. If the men of Dunbar expected Hunter to shoot to kill, they certainly would act likewise. The first impulse of Bull was to gather up his reins, turn Diablo, and send the black stallion across the hills at full speed. Certainly he had been a fool to blunder upon the house in this manner and call out the whole Dunbar force in pursuit.

He hesitated. He was cold with fear, and yet there was an admixture of pleasure in his fear. There is something besides terror in the heart of the wolf as he flees from the pack of hounds. There is a fierce joy in the hunt, even though he is on the dangerous end of the work. For one thing the imp of the perverse tempts the fugitive to dally with danger. And again there are chances to turn swiftly and rend the leading pursuers.

Some of these emotions made Bull Hunter remain quietly on the black stallion, wasting invaluable moments. Diablo himself seemed to understand that he should be off. He was dancing with short steps and tossing his head and snorting softly, as though he would reprove his careless master.

Shouts echoed and reëchoed through the chill, quiet air of the morning. The alarm poured through the barns. It reached the house. Bull saw half a dozen men run out from the building and, standing on the terraces, peer down at him. It would have been the simplest thing in the world to have picked him off with a rifle at that distance. That knowledge at last awakened him. Yet he stayed a single instant longer. Where the great doors at the entrance were swung back, against the darkness of the interior stood a girl dressed in white. Mary Hood, perhaps? At least his heart leaped as though he had been close enough to distinguish the features of her face. He caught off his hat and waved it with a shout, then turned Diablo, and sent him away at full gallop, as a rout of the hunters poured out at him, a dozen men riding close together between two of the outlying sheds.

They wasted no time. The thing to do was either to drop Bull Hunter with a chance shot early in the game or else to accept a long and exhausting chase, for the running powers of Diablo were well known. Therefore the moment they came in view they scattered, pitched their rifles to their shoulders, halted their horses, and opened a close fire. But they found no easy target. Diablo was running as Bull Hunter had taught him to run for the sport of it, taking the hardest course among the trees and dodging back and forth like a jackrabbit, in spite of his burden and his own great size. At that shuttle-like motion of the target, the bullets flew wide. More than one of them sung perilously close to Hunter, but presently he reached denser forest, and the trees were a shield behind him.

At once he called Diablo back to an easy pace. He did not wish to wind the stallion in the first stages of the journey. Moreover, the pursuers were not apt to try to outsprint the great black horse. They were more likely to trust to wearing him down on account of the weight of his rider.

In the meantime the hunt grew in number of voices behind him, and he could hear parties cutting to right and left, spreading out like a fan, so that he would have no chance to escape by doubling back once the chase was fairly under way. By the uproar he guessed rightly that every man on the ranch had taken horse to join in the kill. That would be an easy way to win praise from Jack Hood, the sour old foreman, and money from Hal Dunbar. After the fall of Bull Hunter, Hal Dunbar would ride Diablo.

That thought made Hunter frown. He quickened the pace of the black and so broke out of the forest that surrounded the ranch buildings and came to the wide-rolling meadowlands. What he had suspected was true. The whole body of hunters was not sprinting their horses after him, but one section of four hard riders. Far to his left they were driving their mounts with quirt and spur, and the obvious plan was to send out one group after another, while the main body followed at a moderate pace behind and could come up to overtake the fugitive when Diablo was worn down. It was, after all, the oldest form of jockeying.

One word to Diablo, and he was stretched to full speed. What speed it was! It had been many a week since Bull loosed the big stallion and, as the rush of wind cut into his face, he marveled. Not Bull alone but the whole body of the pursuers gave a shout of wonder, as they crashed out of the forest and saw Diablo sweeping away. He ran as though a lightweight jockey were on his back, and the leading group of riders shook their heads. There was nothing for it but to ride their horses out. There was Hal Dunbar shouting the order as he came out of the forest. He rode a big gray, strong enough to carry his weight but, because of his strength, nearer to a draft horse than a runner. For Hal Dunbar, handsome of face and huge of limb, was as big as Bull Hunter himself. Only one horse in the mountain desert could

165

have carried such bulk with speed, and that horse was the black stallion that now carried Hunter away to safety. Hal Dunbar, spurring in vain to keep up the pace, cursed his horse and Bull Hunter and his men and himself. At that moment he would have paid with the value of half his ranch for the possession of Diablo.

That change of ownership, whether to be accomplished by a bullet or money, was at least postponed. Diablo stepped away from the chase as though the others were standing still. Bull Hunter, glorying in the speed, let him run at his will for half a mile. Then he began to think and called him back to a smooth canter. Even that pace was safely holding the fastest of Dunbar's men, and Dunbar himself was out of sight in the rear.

What ran in the mind of Bull Hunter was that, if every man on the Dunbar place had taken horse to follow him, the ranch house itself was left unprotected. It only remained to cut in behind them, and he could get back and see Mary Hood without danger of interruption.

It was a thought that proved, if Bull was stupid as a strategist, he still had some tactical good sense, but it was not altogether an easy thing to double back. The chase had spread out widely. Far to right and left he saw one little group after another topping the hills and dipping out of view into the hollows, until it seemed that a small army was following him. They rode at a steady, hot pace that would enable them to take instant advantage of any mistake on the part of the fugitive. Not until they struck the mountains, certainly, would he have a chance to double back and, even in the mountains, it would be nearly impossible. So he headed for the nearest foothills.

Twice the ranchmen sprinted from the flanks in an attempt to come up in point-blank range before he could get Diablo away. Twice he forestalled them. But how keenly he missed The Ghost now! The Ghost would have loafed behind and, ranging across the front of the line of the pursuers, would have tried to come

166

to him by short-cuts to report every fresh threat of danger. But there was no wolf dog. Neither was there a Pete Reeve who would have turned in the saddle and kept the pursuers far back with snap rifle shots. Two-thirds of his strength was gone with them; what remained to him was not a large ability to plot, and the only trick he could think of was a childish one in its simplicity.

It consisted in increasing the pace of the black as they approached the foothills, cutting over to one side as though he wished to reach a certain pass well ahead of the right flank of the cowpunchers and then, having drawn them in that direction, trying to cut back across their whole front as soon as he was behind the first screen of hills. It meant calling on Diablo for two bursts of speed, one as he went to the right, and a far greater one as he dashed to the left among the hills, across the whole front of the enemy. But Bull Hunter trusted implicitly to the stallion.

Two miles from the hills he altered his direction sharply to the right and let Diablo out, so that it seemed he was running hard to make the pass. The moment he did it the whole posse drew together and spurted hard, particularly on the right, to gain the pass before him. They might as well have tried to outfoot the wind. Diablo at three-quarters speed gained hand over hand. Before the pass was reached, the squad to the right drew up their horses and began to pump volley after volley toward the pass, in the hope of turning the fugitive.

Bull Hunter, by a very simple expedient, let them think that they had succeeded. He allowed himself to lurch far to the left in the saddle, like a man struck by a bullet, straightened slowly, and then turned, his right arm dangling loosely, and shook his left fist at the posse. After that he turned Diablo toward the hills before him.

A prolonged yell of triumph came ringing and tingling through the air after him. They had winged their quarry, they felt, and the wounded Bull Hunter would do the natural thing and try to put as much country as possible between himself and his pursuers, so that he could dismount and tend to his wound. In this case he would drive the stallion straight across the range.

So they bunched in and followed in that imaginary line, while Hunter, as a matter of fact, as soon as he was behind the first screen of hills, veered the black sharply to the left and, bending far forward in the saddle, let Diablo run as he had never run before. The voice of the hunt rolled to him over the hills, nearer and nearer. He must not be seen, and he must not be heard. He might, for all he knew, be in front of the very middle of the hunt. But he took the chance and, reaching a dense grove of young lodgepole pines, he wedged his way into them and waited.

In less than thirty seconds the first of the hunt appeared well behind him. They made no delay. In the tangle of hills before them a dozen Diablos, with a dozen giant Bull Hunters, might be riding. Straight forward they spurred their mounts. Another group and another followed, drawing in toward the center, spurring hard. Their voices crashed against the opposite slopes and, in another moment, were lost in the confusion of hills. The last group and the closest drove past the clump of lodgepoles, not fifty feet away. Certainly they could have seen the outlines of the horse hidden among the saplings and pinned helpless there, but they had no time for a sideward glance. They were too busy closing in toward the center. Bull Hunter waited until these, too, had passed out of sight, and then he sent Diablo out of the thicket, cantering straight back toward the Dunbar ranch.

# V

## "A MODERN KNIGHT-ERRANT"

It had been Mary Hood who heard the cry: "Bull Hunter is here, up to some deviltry. Everybody out!" It had been she who stood on the verandah, dressed in white, looking down to the giant as he waved his hat. When the hunt had swept after the fugitive, into the forest behind the stables, she had run up to a top window of the big house. Here, with a pair of field glasses, she had followed the chase across the rolling ground, her heart leaping involuntarily in sympathy with the magnificent black and his endangered rider. When they had disappeared, even Hal Dunbar far to the rear, his gray laboring under the weight of his big master, she had turned from the window and gone thoughtfully down to her own room.

She was remembering that first day when Charlie Hunter came to the house of Dunbar, a mighty man indeed, as tall as Hal Dunbar and as bulky, with an even greater suggestion of muscular power. To most people he seemed inhumanly large, but the girl, accustomed all her life to the gigantic Dunbar, looked on the size of this man called Bull Hunter as a more or less common thing. As she recalled it, the stranger on that first day had talked like a child, simply and directly. Hal Dunbar had told her that Hunter was a snake in the grass. And, before the stranger left the house, he had shot down her father, the redoubtable Jack Hood, and left him dangerously wounded. That made him the mortal enemy, not only of Jack Hood, but of all the Dunbars. For Jack Hood was something more than a mere foreman of the great ranch. He had directed it for half his life. His daughter was the prospective wife of Hal, the young owner, and Jack Hood himself was really an integral part of the owner's household.

Yet, thinking of the stranger, she found that she did not hate him as she should. No matter how terrible he might be to men, she felt that she could control him by as small a thing as the lifting of her finger. There was even something horrible in the way in which the Dunbar men had rushed out at the first appearance of the poor fellow, like a pack of wolves.

By this time, perhaps, he was dead. Or his death would come certainly before noon, since no one man could be expected to escape from so many hard riders. And with his death. . . .

At this point in her reflections a deep, smooth bass voice, outside the house, cut in on her thoughts: "Mary Hood! Oh, Mary Hood!"

She knew, though she had only heard that voice on one occasion, that it was Bull Hunter who called. She ran to the window. There he stood, tall and mighty, beside the shining stallion. He was unchanged, only a little leaner and harder and more tanned of face, a trifle more alert in carriage. She looked on him with a shrinking of the heart, as if he were a ghost of the broad daylight. She had seen him, it seemed, only a moment before, riding across the rolling pasture lands with the stream of hunters behind him. Now he stood here alone. She rubbed her eyes; the vision persisted.

"Mary Hood!" he was calling again. "Oh, Mary Hood!"

The madman! Did he not know, if there were one able-bodied man in the house, he would be shot down like a dog were that call heard? Lucky for him that every soul had taken to the saddle for the hunt. Then, remembering that she was alone in the place, she trembled with a new fear, but only for a moment and then she was calm again. She went boldly to the window and leaned out a little. He saw her at once and, for a moment, stared up without speaking. Next he dragged off his sombrero, leaving his hair wild and blowing. It was more than an act of courtesy. There was a touch of worship in the gesture and in the uplifted face that made her uneasy. Then he raised a locket on a chain.

"I have brought back to you," he said, "something that was taken from your father."

For this he had been hunted away like a mad dog. She cried out one grateful word and then hurried downstairs through the big house and onto the verandah. There she paused a moment. Seen from the level he was larger than from above. Since she had first known him, there had come into his face that wild, uneasy look which she had noted once or twice before in outcasts of the mountains. He was holding up the locket and smiling. No matter what he had done, no matter if he had killed every one of the men who had hunted him, she had no cause to fear him. She went down the steps of the verandah very slowly and crossed the terrace. When she had taken the locket, she drew back in surprise at the temerity that had led her to face this man alone.

"I took it from the man who stole it from your father," he said simply. "I knew that you would be unhappy without it."

He talked slowly to the girl, picking his words. With Pete Reeve he used the rough language of the cowpunchers, but the girl appealed in a different way, and there was enough knowledge of good English in him to enable him to respond.

"They shall all know about it," she answered. "They shall all know why you came here, to be driven away like a dog. But how did you break through them? And if you fought my father . . . ?"

"There was no fight. I ran away from them and hid and then came back."

A quiet way of stating a remarkable fact, for how could one man hide from twenty, on ground that the twenty knew like the pages of a book? But she felt at once that he could never be induced to talk about his personal exploits. She found herself smiling at him with a new liking.

"It was so lucky that the thief . . . I mean your friend. . . ." She found herself involved in a hopeless mess of words. Of course the thief was some partner of Bull Hunter's.

"He is a thief," said Bull, "but he is not my friend. I am an honest man . . . so far."

At least he had taken no offense, but she knew that she was crimson. She could tell it by the wonder with which the big man searched her face. But he went on to spare her embarrassment.

"Because I knew him well enough to learn he had this locket in his possession, you thought he was my friend. Even if I live with thieves, I am not a thief, Mary Hood."

"Of course you aren't. And I. . . ."

"I didn't care anything about the locket when he first showed it to me," he continued, "until I saw the face . . . it is very like you." He paused a moment. "It was hard for me to bring it back."

"You have done so much to bring a mere locket back to me?" she asked, thrilling to the thought of it. "Besides the long journey, to face all of Hal's men. . . ."

He broke in as she paused, and he was frowning in his honesty and bewilderment as to the choice of words. "It isn't just to bring you the locket," he went on. "I wanted to see you a lot, and I wanted to see you smile, perhaps, when you took the locket. I guess that's the chief reason."

She was somewhere between blushing and laughter at his painful simplicity.

"Otherwise," he continued, "I could have found someone else to take it back, someone who wouldn't have been in any danger from your friends. So you see what I have done has been quite bad. It made so many men ride so hard."

He waved toward the direction in which the posse had ridden and smiled apologetically at her. She thought at first that there

172

must be hidden sarcasm in the speech, but apparently he was as downright as the broad day. Far from expecting gratitude, he was actually beginning to ask pardon for what he had done.

"Do you dare stay one minute longer?" she asked suddenly.

"Ten minutes, if you will let me."

"They may come back."

"Perhaps."

She smiled with pleasure at his calmness. "You're a rare fellow, Charlie Hunter," she told him. "How long have you ridden this trail?"

"Three days."

"Three days, to bring me this? There isn't another person like you in the world! I'll never forget it."

He shook his head, unhappy at this outburst of eulogy. "There is one very strange thing today," he said to change the subject. "First I come, and twenty men take guns and horses and ride out to meet me. I come again, and there is only one girl without a weapon. You are strange people in this place, Mary Hood."

She had been Mary all her life, and there was something novel and very pleasant in the use of both names together. It endowed her, it seemed, with a new and more unique personality.

"Then we should get along very well," she replied with a smile. "For you are certainly strange among men, Charlie Hunter."

"Yes," he said judicially, "I think I could teach you to like me. I have taught a horse and a wild dog, you see."

She laughed at the comparison. "A wild horse and a wild dog?"

"The dog left me because of another man. But Diablo, you see, is my friend."

"And gentle?"

"As a lamb."

She stretched out her hand. The black stallion sprang far away.

"Gentle!" she exclaimed.

"He has to be introduced," explained Bull. "Now come with me."

He went to Diablo and laid a hand on his neck. The black acknowledged the caress with a quick pricking of his ears and then flattened them again and regarded the timid approach of the girl with angry eyes.

"He's ready to jump at me!" she declared, and stopped.

"He will not. Come slowly . . . steady, Diablo . . . and with your hand out. Touch his nose. If you do that once, he'll remember you, I think."

"Unless he chooses to bite my hand off."

"He will not stir while I talk to him. You see?"

He began to talk smoothly and softly, and the ears of the stallion flickered and came forward, even though Mary began to come close again. Between fear and anger at her coming and pleasure at the soft voice of his master, he trembled from head to foot. Mary Hood was very much afraid, yet she came slowly up until her outstretched hand touched the nose of the stallion. He snorted and winced like a wild horse when the weight of a man first settles on his back but, though his lips twitched, he made no effort to snap.

"Talk to him," said Bull.

Then she talked, as only those who love horses know how, and Bull Hunter left the side of the stallion. Diablo remained motionless, sniffing the hand of the girl.

"Is this the way you always introduce people to him?" she asked when she turned at last to the big man.

"You are the first. Perhaps you are the last. It has made me always happy to be the only one who can go near Diablo, but today, I don't know why, it seems to me that I am happier to share him with someone. See, he is following you."

"No, he is going to you. You're right! You're right! He is coming after me!" She turned and patted the beautiful head of

174

Diablo in delight. "You are a wizard with horses. A true wizard!" she assured him.

"I love them," said Bull Hunter. "That is all. Besides. . . ." He stopped and raised his head. The wind was freshening out of the north, and now it carried to them the sound of a neigh, then the beat of hoofs, far, far away, but distinguishable in the thin mountain air. "They are coming back," said Bull Hunter sadly, "and I must go."

The girl turned angrily toward the approaching sound. Then she touched the arm of Bull Hunter. "You must go, my friend. They have no right to hunt you, but people do not stand on right and wrong on this ranch. I know you have done nothing wrong. You fought my father fairly, and it was his own fault that the fight came at all. I've heard of it all. But now you must go quickly. I shall never forget you and Diablo, but go now!"

He nodded, admitting the gloomy necessity. Yet he still lingered, hunting for words to fit an idea that had just come to him. "There is only one thing more," he said. "I shall miss the locket, Mary Hood, more than you can understand."

"What do you mean?"

"There are lonely times in the mountains, you see. There are times so lonely that a picture is just like another person. It is company. You understand?"

There was no mystery in it. A child would have known. His worship of her was in his eyes. The girl flushed, pitying him, and excited and proud of the tribute. "Of all the strange men who have ever lived," she said, "you are the strangest. You have ridden three days and risked being shot in order to ask me if you can keep a picture?"

"In order to give you the picture and ask it back from your hands," he corrected her. "That is very different. I can find anybody's picture and keep it. But that gives me no right. You see, that painter was very cunning. He put a smile on your face

175

that might be because you were very happy with a friend, or riding a horse, or dreaming. If you give me the picture, Mary Hood, when I look at it, I shall feel you may at that very moment be thinking of me. That is simple, but it means a good deal to me. Will you let me have it?"

She dropped it into his hand. "You have earned it a thousand times over, and it makes me proud to have you want it."

The outburst of frankness left her afraid that she had said too much. But Bull Hunter was too busy examining the locket and putting it away to notice her confusion.

"It is not to be a gift," he declared. "You may want something done, somewhere, somehow. Let me do it in exchange for this."

She nodded, smilingly excited again. All the time she wondered that this big, simple fellow could amuse her so much and give her a peculiar uplifted feeling. It was a novel idea, this purchase by service. It was a scheme worthy of the old days of knight-errantry, and naturally she thought of jousts and battles. Then the inspiration struck her that was to give her many a heartache before all was done.

"Charlie Hunter," she said, "if you want to earn the locket, find the man who stole it and turn him over to the law. Would you do as much as that?"

As she turned, the slant sun of the young morning glinted in her eyes, blinding her, so that she did not see the sudden change in his expression.

"Mary Hood," he answered after a little pause, "I've sat by the camp fire with that man, and I've eaten his bacon and bread."

The disappointment made her sigh.

"But if you want him taken. . . ."

"I do!"

"Then," said Bull Hunter, "I'll do my best. Good bye. Perhaps I shall see you again. . . ."

He was on his horse before she was able to answer. "But of

176

course I shall see you again!"

"Who knows?" answered Charlie Hunter from the back of Diablo. "There are always two ways a man's trail may end."

Leaving her breathless, he touched the flank of Diablo with his heel, and the great black swept him down the terraces.

# VI

## "THE GHOST'S PROGRESS"

Meanwhile the great wolf dog, The Ghost, more wolf indeed than dog, had fled through the night without pause. In his mind all was a sad jumble. He had fled from the call of his master for a good and definite reason. He had seen clearly from the beginning that it was the will of the master that he become kind to men and the creatures of men. That scent, which he loathed and dreaded the most, the scent of man, so keen in the wind and so strong underfoot, making the hair of all beasts of prey prickle and ruff up, that very scent, according to the apparent will of the master, was the thing which should make The Ghost kindly to those who possessed it. Their servants he must not kill; themselves he must regard with awe.

Such had been the lesson which The Ghost had learned painfully and slowly. Sheer weight of loneliness and longing for something of his kind had made him approach the mongrel cur that belonged to Dunkin. It was the greatest concession The Ghost could have made. He knew well that he could have slashed the throat of the dog from ear to ear in ten seconds. He knew he could outwit and outrun him. But fate threw him into the necessity of making friends with such a base creature, and he made the best of it. All the time that he was moving about the mongrel, making his advances, he was keeping an eye and an ear for applause from his master. That applause was not forthcoming. When, finally, he decided that the master had lost his interest in this particular cur of a dog and made up his mind that the beast might be killed with impunity for his ungracious reception, even at the moment when he had the work well under way, he had been seized in the midst of his attack, swung into the air, and dashed down upon the ground. Truly this was an irony. It was more. It was a burning shame. He had been laughed at by the companion of the master in the midst of his shame. If there was justice, why had not the master smitten that man for mocking The Ghost? There was no justice. The mind of the master was changed and poisoned, and the world was full of emptiness and bitter heartache for The Ghost.

Therefore he fled through the night at his best long-distance pace. He discovered ere long that his muscles were not what they had once been. He had done no real running in the company of Bull Hunter. To one who could kill, eat full, sleep, and do an easy fifty miles, all within the space of twenty-four hours, what was a paltry thirty miles a day at the end of which he was fed by the master? The pads of his feet were soft. His wind was not sound. The story of the trail, told in a hundred and a thousand scents, was dim and often almost illegible, for his nostrils had been clogged and dulled by the soot of camp fires. Decidedly he was not his old self. He could have mastered any two wolves on the ranges in fair fight but, nevertheless, he was not The Ghost that of old had been the terror of the mountains. Neither could he give a single mind to his work and his place. When the owl swooped low and hooted a greeting, or when the nighthawk swung past on silent brushing wings, he had neither howl nor upward glance with which to welcome them. They had been his brothers in the law of slaughter once. But now, between him and them, there was the shadow of the man who had been his master. And between him and the freedom of the mountains was the memory of the man. The voice of Bull Hunter still called him in the wind and made him slink close to the ground for a step or two.

Had he only feared the giant he could have rejoiced. But he feared and loved the man at once. Therefore his brute mind was in torment. One thing was certain: the dogs would not accept him, and Bull Hunter would not accept the wolves. Between wolf and man he must take his choice, and he hunted now for his kind. Many a scent came to his nostrils of rabbit and chipmunk and birds and coyotes and foxes, and once he followed for half a dozen miles a promising scent, only to find at the end of the trail a little prairie wolf that fled madly at his coming.

The Ghost turned upwind in disgust from such a quarry. He gave himself a mile or two of terrific running to make him forget the shame of his mistake, and at the end of it, without warning scent, he dropped suddenly upon the thing he sought. Half a dozen lobos fed on the carcass of two newly slain calves in which the life was still hot. The moon was a dim sickle cutting through the trees on the peak above. By its uncertain light The Ghost viewed his fellows and was glad at heart. He dropped upon his haunches and gave voice to the hunting call that had more than once passed, wailing and shivering, through the mountains and made apprehensive ranchers reach for their rifles and curse the darkness which screened the marauder. But far better was it known to the other big loafer wolves. More than one had felt his teeth, and there were few of the others who had not seen him fight. One bay was enough to send the six wolves in the hollow leaping away from their meat, apprehensive and on the alert.

The Ghost looked on with immense satisfaction and, having stared his full and seen that not one of the band dared go back to its food until his orders were known, he dropped down into the hollow at a lazy jog trot. When he came near, he saw that there were three youngsters, two females, and a scarred old veteran of a leader. Few loafer wolves could gather a pack to themselves, but this one-eared hero, in his strength and wisdom, had proved the exception. He made a pace forward from his companions as The Ghost came to a halt over the first carcass and stared about him. But the forward step of the leader was not a challenge. It was merely a feeble attempt to assert his dignity in the eyes of his followers and, knowing that, The Ghost despised a fight which would have been murder. Besides, he was too wise to battle for pleasure, knowing full well that the weakest yearling wolf may ruin the fiercest of his elders by a lucky bite that severs a tendon.

However, it was well to assert his mastery, even with the weak. It might be his pleasure to lead this pack and, if that proved to be his will, he might as well begin now. A hungry yearling ventured toward the second carcass. The Ghost sent him back with a terrible snarl. The yearling leaped back with his tail between his legs, and The Ghost sauntered carelessly toward the body of the second dead calf.

He had barely reached it when a low-pitched snarl from the old leader made him stop, quivering. For that whining snarl of fear and rage meant, in wolf talk, man. The Ghost jerked his head to one side, but the wind carried to his nostrils only the pure scent of the grass and the trees. He glanced back at the others and started in astonishment. They had formed in a loose semicircle: One Ear in the center, with a female on either side, and on the flanks were the yearlings. They moved slowly forward, crouching low to the ground, with necks and heads stretched straight out, their noses pointing toward him. Now from every throat came that same whining snarl that meant man.

The Ghost glared in astonishment. Was it possible that they were about to attack him *en masse*, as wolves attack a dog? He settled back as if for a leap, and at once the six divided and crouched lower, but they still advanced. He sent his longest and greatest hunting cry, ringing and filling the hollow. Though they paused until the last echo died away, the advance began again the next moment.

Then he understood. It was the scent of man that lingered on him. More than that perhaps he had learned from his society with men the ways of a dog. With fear and rage The Ghost watched that silent advance of his fellows. Suddenly one of the she-wolves coughed and darted at him to catch his flank. The Ghost sprang high and far. His aim was not the she-wolf, but the cunning old leader who had kept discreetly in the background. High over him sprang The Ghost. It was a trick he had learned in his youth in a battle with a terrible old wolf hound that nearly cost him his life. For the hound had the art of vaulting above an enemy and snapping as he went by, an improvement on the old wolf method of cutting from the side.

It worked now like a charm. The teeth of The Ghost sank into the back of One Ear's neck, and the shock spun The Ghost straight over in mid-air, before his teeth tore loose. Yet he landed on his feet, and he landed running. To make one attack in the face of any odds was the part of valor. To run with all his might from six hostile members of his own kind was the part of extreme wisdom. And The Ghost was wise.

The yearlings, who are sprinters *par excellence*, nearly caught him in the first two hundred yards, but after that he drew smoothly away. One Ear himself was too badly hurt to follow, and the she-wolves quickly lost interest. In a mile the pursuit ended, and The Ghost drew his pace to the tireless lope.

He had escaped a great danger. He had inflicted a severe wound without return. That, in the wolf code, is the greatest happiness. In spite of his triumph the heart of The Ghost was aching. He had been outcast by his brothers.

181

He came on a flock of sheep on the windward side of a hill, bedded down in comfort. Ordinarily he killed cattle only, but these sheep meant living creatures in his way, and The Ghost hated all things that lived. He charged them like a terrible shadow. The neck of the first shepherd dog was broken before he could utter a single howl of warning. The foreleg of a second was crushed. The Ghost rushed among the sheep, slaughtering on either side and before him as he went. One bite apiece was sufficient for that expert slaughterer. The shepherd himself was up, wailing with rage and fear and firing random bullets in the air. They only increased the satisfaction of The Ghost, for the very sheep that he was killing protected him from the danger of the man. He rushed through the last bleating group and was over the hill, drenched with slaughter but still unsatisfied.

He reached the buildings of a squatter a few miles further on, pitifully small sheds in the midst of the wilderness of mountains. Here, in a little outer corral, he found a sleek young two-year-old colt asleep. The Ghost leaped the fence and then paused to grin at the simplicity of the thing. It needed only one soft growl to waken the colt and bring him in terror to his feet, still blind with sleep. Then he could dive under and cut the throat of the horse with a bite.

Pausing to enjoy the thing in prospect, The Ghost cleansed his fur then circled the colt slowly. The stupid creature was so deeply in sleep that The Ghost could sniff within a fraction of an inch of his hide without alarming him. Still he delayed the snarl that was to rouse the victim for the slaughter. He sat down on his haunches with lolling tongue and pondered. It was strange, this reluctance to kill. Continually in the back of his brain was the thought of black Diablo and the many games that they had played together. Of course it had been most perfect when the master had played with them. He knew how to direct the game. In truth those had been happy days.

He was an outcast from them. He had fled from the master's voice and, having once offended, he would never be accepted again. Even so, he was also an outcast from the society of other wolves. Then what place remained to him?

He started up to make the kill and, as he did so, the colt raised his head and looked idly about him. It was a head very like the head of Diablo when The Ghost had slipped out into the corral on many a night to touch noses with the stallion. While he was crouched for the spring, The Ghost felt his muscles relax.

At length, as noiselessly as he had come, he slipped from the corral and fled away across the hills. It was the beginning of a period of ceaseless wandering. He killed irregularly, joylessly, only for food. Neither did it matter what was his prey, but more and more there was a growing distaste for the creatures of man. Now he caught squirrels and chipmunks and rabbits, beggarly prey for The Ghost as he had once been. Alas, he was changed! There was one single instant of joy, a battle with a lone veteran of a wolf whom he met on a narrow trail along a cañon side. That fight ended with his foe toppling a thousand feet below to destruction, and The Ghost went on.

One who watched him would have known that he was hunting. Of that The Ghost was unaware; he only knew that his heart ached steadily, that his muscles were growing lean, and his skin was hanging in folds. For it was the old tragedy of the wilderness. Wild creatures that have been once tamed can never be truly wild again. The chain with which men hold their slaves has no weight. It is the mind, and this chain can never be broken.

While The Ghost hunted for happiness in the mountains where he had been a king, roaming in great and ever widening circles, chance brought him the explanation at which he himself could never have arrived. For, as he lay under a tree one day, a dust cloud, far down a winding trail, dissolved into a horseman. When the horseman drew near, he saw the glint of the sun on the shining black charger. Then a veering of the wind brought him an old, old scent.

The Ghost leaped to his feet. There was something like a great thirst in his throat, and yet the coldest, clearest water that ever bubbled in a mountain spring could never have satisfied it. Presently he sat back on his haunches, and the long, weird, heart-chilling wolf yell went echoing down the mountainside.

In response the sun flashed on a naked rifle barrel, as the rider swung it into place. The Ghost winced away. Well he knew the meaning of that glimmer of steel, wavering back and forth in a straight line that steadied to a point. Yet he knew the hand on the gun also, and he rose mournfully and raised his head to wait for the end. Twice, blinking at that point of light on the barrel, as the rider drew the bead, he thought the end had come, and then the rifle was lowered, and the hand of the man went up.

A voice was calling him down the wind, a voice that made his heart thunder in response. The Ghost fled like the wind to meet Bull Hunter. Three swift circles he made around the horse and rider, with Diablo whinnying a soft welcome. Then he ran to them and placed his forepaws on the knee of the master and licked his hand.

He knew that the other hand stroked his battle-scarred head, while the voice, speaking as kindly as ever, was saying to him: "Old Pete Reeve was right. You're like him, partner. You're no dog, and you're no wolf, but you belong in between. Just where, darned if I know, but you and me'll work it out together. If only I could do the same for Pete."

# VII

## "THE CHALLENGE"

It was far north on the mountain desert, in one of those towns that grow up like weeds and die like weeds in the West, according as lumber and mining camps are opened and closed and as the cattle centers change. Viewed by the hawk's eye from above, the town was merely a rough collection of shacks whose roofs sent back the sunshine in a myriad of heat waves. The houses were weathered to the color of the desert, a deadly drab. Some of them had been painted once or twice, but dry heat in summer and fierce storms in winter peeled up the paint and soaked it away. It was not a town in the desert; it was part of the desert, called by grace a town. Yet to its inhabitants it was a haven of refuge. Under those low roofs was shade, and the floor could be drenched with water many times a day for the sake of coolness.

Dunkin and Pete Reeve sat on the verandah, freshly drenched from buckets. Each took his ease, tilted far back in a chair, the soles of his feet braced against separate pillars. In that position the hotel proprietor found them as he came sweating up the steps.

"When I asked for the hotel mail," he said, "the postmaster give me this letter for you, Mister Hardy."

Then he passed on into the hotel. As for Hardy, alias Dunkin, he sat as one stunned, turning the letter over and over in his hands.

"But it can't be for me," he declared to Reeve. "Must be some other John Hardy around here . . . a real one, I mean. Nobody that would write to me knows I'm here."

"It's meant for you, right enough," Reeve assured him. "If there was another Hardy around here, wouldn't they know about

185

him? Open up and let's hear the good news."

Dunkin, still shaking his head, opened the letter, and read aloud:

I've been looking for you a long time, Dunkin, and just the other day a gent blew into town and told me about a fellow named Hardy. What he said tallied pretty closely with you. When he spoke about Pete Reeve, I was sure it was you.

So I'm writing this letter to let you know why I want to see you. For reasons I can't explain, it's come to the point where one of us has to go down, and naturally I'd rather that one should be you. I don't care how you want to fight, on horse or foot, or with rifles or Colts or knives.

I'm over in Tuckertown now, the eighteenth, and I'll wait here till the morning of the day after tomorrow. If you don't come looking for me by that time, I'll come looking for you.

Say hello to Pete Reeve for me.

Charles Hunter

Dunkin finished the letter in a staggering voice. He laughed, crumpled it up, threw it on the floor, picked it up and unraveled the tangle of paper again, and finally launched a stream of tremendous curses.

"I'll go to Tuckertown for him," he said at length. "When I get through with him, there won't be enough left to fill a coffee pot. But what's happened to him? Has he gone crazy?"

"He always hated you," said Pete Reeve with a surprising lack of emotion.

"Say, I think you're on his side."

"Sure I am, except that he's hunting you, while you and me

186

happen to be partners. The law of the range stands that a gent has to back up his partner. No, Dunkin, if Bull comes for you while you and me are on the trail, he'll have to drop both of us in order to get one."

"Thanks," said Dunkin, "but I don't need no help. I'll settle the business of this gent in a jiffy. After I say one word, the buzzards can finish the sentence."

He enjoyed his own little joke so hugely that he almost laughed himself back into a good humor. But he came out of his laughter sharply and, rising from the chair, he said: "He's waiting for me. Want to come along to Tuckertown and see the party?"

"The party is more likely to come off right here," said Reeve gravely. "This is the twentieth, and he's due to come. His letter must have got hung up in the mails some way. It's only eight miles to Tuckertown."

"Why did he write, the fool? Why not come over like a man and give me a dare? I've always hated him, too."

"Even a snake gives you a rattle before he hits you," said Reeve. "Bull wanted to give you fair warning of what was coming. If I was you, Dunkin, I'd take that warning and start riding."

"I'm not afraid of him," replied Dunkin. "You say he's pretty good with a gun, but you think everything he does is pretty good. Well, I'll give him a try. What you say about Bull Hunter don't count."

"Maybe not," assented the withered little man. "He's the best friend I've got, the best friend any man could have. He'd give his life for me. That's why I want you to run for it, Dunkin. If you stay, I got to stay with you and face my old partner with a gun. If you run, I'll run with you and show you a way to get off . . . for a while anyway."

"For a while? You talk like this gent Hunter was sure to get me."

"He is," answered Reeve with the same disconcerting calm.

187

"In spite of you, if it takes him ten years for the job. Dunkin, take another think and put a saddle on your hoss and go."

There was something so convincing in Reeve's manner of speaking that Dunkin actually started across the verandah, but he halted after a few steps and turned back. "I'll see him hung first," he declared at length. "Here we are in the only part of the range where you ain't known . . . where we can work with a free hand. I won't be turned out by any thick head like Hunter. Reeve, we're going to stick, that's final. If you want to give me a hand ag'in' this gent, I'll say pretty frank that I'll be glad to have you. If you don't want to help, I'll stay and face him alone."

Reeve made a gesture of surrender. "I've told you what I'll do already," he said, "and I'll stick by that. But I'd rather be dead myself than shoot a bullet at Hunter."

Then he sank deeply in his chair and closed his eyes. Great was the temptation that he passed through. To him big Charlie Hunter was more than a friend, he was almost a son. But the law of the range was explicit and unalterable. A man's partner must be valued as his right hand. And there was justice behind the law. In the peril of the mountains and the desert a man's partner must be trusted as himself, or it meant ruin for both of them. One glutton at the canteen could drink up the supply of two and cause the death of both by thirst; the coward, who ran from a danger instead of standing to face it, could cause two deaths.

There was justice in the law and, though Pete Reeve did not see the justice at the moment, he was prepared, nevertheless, to accept the letter of the law. Before the day wore out, perhaps, he would face Bull Hunter and fight him to the death.

He had hardly made up his mind when a boy, riding horseback on a fleet pony, dashed down the street and ran to the verandah with a scared face. "They's a gent coming with a wolf!" he called

188

to them. "A gent with an honest-Injun loafer wolf trotting along in front of him."

It brought Pete Reeve and Dunkin to their feet.

"He's here," whispered Dunkin. "Are you with me, Pete?"

"I'm with you. But the wolf? Has The Ghost come back to him?"

"Must be, because . . . yes, that's The Ghost."

Around the bend of the single street glided the gray form of the big lobo. He paused with head erect, the broad wistful face turning inquiringly to either side. Then, from behind, came the master on the tall black stallion, and The Ghost moved on. The strange little procession brought people to windows and doors, staring in amazement tinged with fear. More than one man reached for his gun at the sight of the wolf dog. Just across the street from the hotel, a woman scolded her children hastily back into the house.

Straight to the verandah of the hotel came The Ghost, reared, placed his forepaws on the edge of the porch, and stared long and earnestly into the face of Dunkin. It was as though he had picked out by foreknowledge the enemy of his master, though doubtless Bull Hunter had taught him the scent of the enemy. Then the great animal slipped down and returned like a silent shadow to his master. By this time Hunter had seen them. He halted his horse and turned in the saddle toward them.

"Now," said Dunkin, his whole body trembling with nervous anxiety, "now I'll make my play."

"If you do, it's murder," said Reeve. "Bull Hunter won't make a gun play in this town full of people, and he don't expect you to try. Look! He's waving to us. If he meant quick action, d'you think he'd take his hand that far away from his gun? Never in the world."

Bull shouted a cheery greeting to them and then swung out of the saddle and strode toward them. If he looked huge in the saddle, he seemed more mountainous than ever, walking on foot. Diablo followed at his heels like a dog. Pete Reeve ran to meet him and wrung his hands. He looked like a midget before the giant, yet if any man of the mountain desert had been asked to pick the more formidable of the two, he would have picked the midget without a moment's hesitation. For, at this time in his career, Bull Hunter was known to be huge, but very little else was widely known about him, while the fame of Pete Reeve had spread far and wide.

They walked on together toward the verandah, laughing happily. At the verandah they met Dunkin, and the laughter stopped.

"I sent you a letter," said Bull Hunter mildly, "asking you to come to meet me in Tuckertown. But I guess the letter didn't come, Dunkin."

"It came, right enough," answered Dunkin. "And I'm ready to meet you anywhere. The only reason I didn't come was because you ain't worth that much trouble, Bull. Besides, the letter just got here. It must have been held up. For the rest I've hated the sight of you for a long time, and I'm glad we're going to have it out now. Mighty glad."

"I'm not," answered Bull. "I've never liked you, Dunkin, but I've never hated you."

"Only enough to want to pump me full of lead, eh?" asked the robber.

"Lead? Shooting?" asked Bull in mild surprise. "Why, man, I'm not going to kill or try to kill you."

"You ain't? Then what is it that you aim to try to do with me?"

"Take you alive and turn you over to the law. That's my job."

It brought a gasp from both Reeve and Dunkin.

"Son," said Dunkin hotly, "you get one chance in three of

dropping me with a bullet in a fair fight. But you nor nobody else has got a chance in a million of taking me alive!"

"Maybe I ain't," answered Bull mildly, "but I'll die trying it."

"While you're trying," went on Dunkin coldly, "remember that you got two on your hands, not one. When you get me, you got to get Pete Reeve first."

It was a thunderbolt to Bull Hunter. He made a gesture like a blind man toward the little gunfighter.

"Pete," he exclaimed, "are you with him in this?"

Pete Reeve dropped his head. "It's an old law," he said bitterly, "and it always has to work. I'm on the trail with Dunkin, Bull. In a month or two I may be away from him, and then you're free to tackle him alone. While I'm with him, my grub is his grub, and my hoss is his hoss, and my gun is his gun. That's the way it works, and that's the way it's always got to work, or else they'll be no more living in the West. I guess that's the straight of it."

"That may be the way with you," said Bull Hunter, "but no matter where I was, I'd never lift a hand ag'in' you. Not for love or money, Pete. It changes things a good deal."

He went a half step closer to Dunkin. "There's one thing new I got to tell you, Dunkin. I started out wanting just to take you alive. I'm beginning to want to kill you. And I'm beginning to think I will." His broad forehead wrinkled with thought. "I'd forgive any man a lot, but never the one that turned Pete Reeve ag'in' me. Dunkin, watch yourself. I'm going to follow you and Pete, when you leave town. I'm going to watch my chance. I'll wait maybe a year, but I'll get you away from Pete and tie you like a bale of hay and take you to town to the sheriff. Keep that in your head, my friend."

Dunkin attempted to sneer, but his lips trembled beyond control. He tried to laugh, but the sound dried up in his throat.

Then Bull Hunter turned on his heel and strode away, the thick dust of the street squirting up like steam from the heavy stamping of his feet.

"What's come over him?" asked Dunkin. "He used to be a thick-headed kid. He seems to have growed up in the last few weeks."

"I dunno," said Pete Reeve wearily. "He's waking up. It's partly a woman, I guess, and it's partly that he thinks I've failed him."

# VIII

## "LOSS AND GAIN"

That night after supper the spirits of Dunkin rose perceptibly. "It's all bluff, Pete," he said to his companion as he lighted a cigarette after the big tin cup of coffee that finished his meal. "If Hunter meant business, he'd have stayed right here and watched us till we left town. But he's disappeared. It's all bluff. When he seen that you were with me, he lost his nerve."

"Not if ten like me were with you," answered the imperturbable Reeve. "He's cached himself away in some shack near the town, and he's watching the trails from there. But there's one way we might give him the slip. He probably doesn't expect us to move away from town for a couple of days. If we make a jump in the middle of tonight, we might take him by surprise and get by."

Dunkin glanced twice at his friend to make sure that he was serious. The idea of Pete Reeve stealing away by night was not in the books, but there was no doubting the seriousness of the little man. "You know this gent a pile better than I do," said

Dunkin at last. "So you run the party, and I'll do what you say."

Accordingly they went to sleep early, with orders to be wakened a little after midnight. At that hour they were up and in the saddle. There could not have been a worse night for travel. A chill wind was coming down from the higher northern mountains, carrying a piercing drizzle of rain and, though their slickers turned the force of it, it found crevices here and there, and the sharp wind drove the rain to the skin.

Dunkin steadily cursed the weather and Bull Hunter. Twice he begged the little man to turn back with him to the hotel and bid defiance to the giant. Reeve was inflexible in his purpose.

"If we get over the trail of the Culver Pass," he said, "we'll be in country that Hunter doesn't know, and he'll be at sea. Keep that hoss moving."

So they plodded steadily over the road that the rain was quickly turning to slush. They drifted down the main street to the outer limits of the town, unseen and unheard, for the drum of rain on the roofs covered all minor sounds. In the open country the rain was merely a swishing sound on the sand and dead grass. The air was filled with the scent of the arid soil, as it greedily drank up the moisture, and there were steady whispering noises like promises of the green life that was to come.

By the road just outside the village they passed some low clumps of shrubbery. "Suppose he were lying out in there?" suggested Pete Reeve. "If he was, he'd see us pass quick enough."

"Too low to cover a man as big as him," said Dunkin confidently. "Besides, nobody but a crazy man would lie out in this rain. Pete, you're all wrong about this. We don't need to hurry. Bull Hunter is asleep and snoring. We're just fading out, and he'll never find us beyond the Culver Pass."

"I'll believe that when we're safely over," answered Pete

with unshaken gloom.

Indeed, at that very moment there was a watcher in the shrubbery who heard their voices. Not a man but a great wolf dog was crouched under a bush that formed an almost perfect tent above him to shed the rain. As the two horsemen passed, he glided across the road to the leeward side and skulked swiftly from bush to bush, taking the scent.

Presently he appeared to be satisfied and shot back toward the town. The town itself was not his goal, however. Skirting around behind it, with the sand scuffing up behind him from his hurrying paws, he came to a wretched group of trees on the far side of the village and close to the trail where it entered the town. Among these trees he plunged and came presently on the great bulk of Hunter, sitting with his back against a tree, wrapped in a capacious slicker. All night he had kept patient watch. Now the cold nose of the wolf dog touched his hand.

As he turned his head, The Ghost retreated, looking back over his shoulder. At that the master rose hastily, flung a saddle on Diablo, and was instantly underway. His stratagem had been simple enough. In the shed behind the hotel he had taken the wolf to the horses of Reeve and Dunkin to freshen their scent in his nose. At dusk he had posted the big animal on the far side of the town. He himself guarded the only other way of entering or leaving the town. He could trust The Ghost to report. Many a time before he had used the cunning hunting instincts of the loafer wolf and taught him to play this very game of tag with Pete Reeve. Now it stood him in good stead.

They went at a mild trot through the village. As soon as they hit the open trail beyond, he gave a short whistle that sent The Ghost bounding away in the lead to disappear instantly behind the thick curtain of night and the rain. After a time he himself let Diablo take his head for a burst of strong running, until a sudden figure shot into view again. It was The Ghost returning

194

to apprise his master that he had located the fugitives and was keeping in touch with them.

As he returned, The Ghost gamboled about the rider, leaping high and snapping in pretended ferocity at the nose of Diablo. For this game of hunting was the greatest joy in The Ghost's life with his master. Playing it, he had a faint taste of the old free days when he was king of the mountains. There was an added joy in playing it with Bull Hunter. For when he ran a quarry to the ground, were it grizzly or mountain lion, the rifle of the master was always sure to make the kill. Odds ceased to exist and, with the master in sight, The Ghost would have attacked at command a whole host of lions.

His task this night was far simpler; it was ridiculously easy for him. As the connecting link he raced back and forth, coming just within hearing of the splash of water and mud under the feet of the horses of the fugitives and then loped back to communicate news of his industry. One word was all the reward he wanted. Sometimes he stopped to touch noses with Diablo; sometimes he took a brief vacation and, racing through some neighboring field or wood, he made short detours along the scents of wet trails, not yet drowned, then back to play the game for his master.

Of course it was invaluable to Bull Hunter to have this assistant spy. He himself could linger far behind, entirely out of danger of being heard or seen by the men he trailed. As he rode along, secure on the back of Diablo, even when the trail became most treacherous, he tried to order some plan of attack. It was by no means simple. To attack Dunkin alone would have been nothing. To attack him and try to take him alive was a thousand times more difficult and necessitated a surprise. To surprise him while Pete Reeve rode in his company was practically impossible.

The rain ceased while he was in the midst of these reflections. The northern wind, which had blown the storm upon them, was succeeded by a brisk western breeze that whipped the sky clean of clouds in a few moments and left the big mountains and the stars and the blue-black depths of the sky above him. All around there was a crinkling sound of the thirsty earth, drinking.

It also meant that Bull Hunter could see his surroundings more clearly. They were rapidly climbing toward the heart of that narrow defile known as the Culver Pass. The trail that wound through it sometimes climbed along the side of the cliff with barely enough room for one horseman. The cliffs themselves dropped down to the bed of the swift torrent that had cut the gulch. Ordinarily a trail would have been made on the bank of the stream itself. But it was impossible to travel over the enormous boulders that were strewn on either side of the water, and the trail was forced to follow a very precarious course.

It would be impossible to attack the two who rode in front on such a trail, for they were probably in single file with the redoubtable Pete Reeve himself in the rear to guard against precisely such an attack. Yet it was very necessary to stop the two before they got out of the pass and reached the broken country beyond, a bad stretch through which pursuit would be very difficult, if not impossible.

Bull Hunter reviewed his means of attack. There was the rifle slung in the scabbard; there was the heavy revolver at his hip. Neither was really available if he hoped to take Dunkin alive. There was also the lariat and that, in a way, was a weapon of another sort and precisely adapted to such a capture. With that thought the idea came to Bull Hunter.

He put Diablo at the first slope that he reached leading toward the summit of the cliff upon that side. It was a desperate climb. The Ghost went on ahead, pointing the way in the most effectual manner possible. For he knew intimately the capacities of Diablo when it came to climbing, and he scouted on, exploring every dangerous section and coming back to show the way up the easiest course. Even then Bull Hunter could not stay in the saddle and hope to make the climb. He had to dismount before they had gone a hundred yards.

A little farther on it was necessary to remove the saddle from Diablo. Bull Hunter toiled and moiled up the wet hill, carrying the heavy saddle. Diablo struggled valiantly in his wake, with The Ghost as the vanguard.

Finally, as the gray dawn appeared, they reached the crest. Hunter saddled again in frantic haste. It had taken incredibly long to make that short climb. Looking down into the dizzy shadows of the cañon, he wondered how he had made it at all. Perhaps the fugitives would have passed out of Culver Pass by this time and were already riding into the comparative safety of the badlands beyond.

There was an immediate reward for the climb. The surface of the crest was a long stretch of almost level plateau. It was impossible to ride at more than a walk along the trail by the cañon. Up here a horse could run at full gallop, but Bull put Diablo only to half his full speed, and even so the wind felt like a gale in his face.

One gesture told The Ghost what his part in the business must be. He rushed on ahead, swinging along the verge of the drop toward the gulch and scanning the trail as it wound along the cliff. With anxiety Bull Hunter noted the wolf dog still kept running on at full speed, though the end of the pass had almost come. He was beginning to despair when The Ghost changed his lope to a slouching trot, hanging his nose close to the edge of the cliff. The dog had found them, and the heart of Bull Hunter leaped again.

He took Diablo in a wide detour, so that the sound of the galloping might not come to the two on the narrow cliff trail. Swinging in ahead of The Ghost again, he flung himself from the saddle, whipped the lariat from its place, and ran to a point of vantage. It was a point where the cliff jagged out in a triangle, and the trail followed that conformation in an elbow bend.

There had been more than one tragedy at this point on the trail. Of this Bull Hunter was ignorant. He only knew that angling rock would mask, from him who came second, whatever happened to the first rider. He could only pray that the first rider, as he surmised, would be Dunkin. If Pete Reeve came first, it would be impossible to make the attack he had planned. The terrible little gunfighter would be able to wheel in the saddle at the first alarm and end everything with one bullet.

Bull Hunter lay flat on his stomach at the cliff edge and looked down, waiting. The drop to the narrow trail — and how precariously narrow it seemed! — was a full eighteen feet, and the rocky face to the crest was weatherworn to a glassy smoothness. So much he noted with satisfaction and then drew the rope up beside him and shook out the noose.

Below and beyond stretched a marvelous view of the badlands, a chopped and broken country, still filled with pools of night. Over them the sky rose in a lovely arch, so near that it seemed to Bull he could stand up and touch the solid blue. Day was coming fast, and it seemed to him that he could hear inarticulate noises of life awakening, though it was only the first faint morning breeze that was springing up. But now, down the trail, he heard unmistakable sounds of human voices, traveling toward him quickly. They seemed already on him and about to turn the curve, though the figure of The Ghost, slouching along the cliff, assured him that they were still a little distance off.

What they were saying he could not distinguish, for a thousand echoes confused the syllables. But now his attention was fixed on The Ghost, coming slowly closer to the elbow turn. The circle was at hand. Who rode first, Reeve or Dunkin? Success or failure depended on the approaching figure. Then he saw a horse's head nodding as he came wearily around the turn, and then the level neck, and now the horn of the saddle. Dunkin rode into view! Bull Hunter cast one swift glance upward, an involuntary thanksgiving. His grip settled more firmly on the rope. Dunkin raised his head. Bull's first emotion was to shrink back, but he remembered that a moving object quickly attracts attention. Dunkin was so far from expecting a human face above him that he probably would not see. There he came, looking straight up, it seemed, into the eyes of Hunter, but apparently all he noticed was the blueness of the sky.

He dropped his head to curse a stumble of his horse, and at that instant Bull dropped the noose. There was one startled — "What the thunder?" — from Dunkin as the circle dropped about his waist. Bull heaved up with all his strength, and the noose, sliding up under the strain, came taut and settled closely, just under the arms of the victim. He was wrenched from the saddle at the first heave, and his yell of amazement and terror filled, it seemed to Bull Hunter, the whole width of the cañon.

An answering shout came, but Bull noted gratefully that it came from beyond the elbow turn. In the meantime he settled to his work. Hand over hand he whipped the screaming Dunkin up toward him. A frightened glance upward showed Dunkin that his persecutor stood above in the form of Hunter, and a fresh cry rose from his lips.

Soon the head of Pete Reeve's horse, nodding quickly from his trot, appeared in view, and then came Pete himself with poised gun. But his eyes were fastened down the trail at his own level. As he glanced up with a shout of amazement at the spinning form of Dunkin, as the latter swung in mid-air, the victim was swung over the edge of the cliff. One fraction of an instant too late the bullet from Reeve's gun hummed over the head of the giant.

Hunter gave no heed. Neither did he hear the frantic cursing of the little man below, as he vainly strove to climb that glassy surface of the cliff. His attention was too much taken by the struggle with Dunkin.

It was very brief. In one mighty hand he gathered the wrists of the robber behind his back and tied them securely. When the captive called afresh for help, Bull ground his face mercilessly into the dirt. One dose of that treatment sufficed. Then Bull, carrying his trussed man over one arm, climbed into the saddle on Diablo. He rode the black close to the cliff.

"Pete!" he called. "Pete Reeve!"

The shouts of the little man, as he strove to climb the rock wall, ceased abruptly.

"Pete," said Bull, "I had to do it. You dunno how hard it was to go ag'in' you, but I had to do it. Will you forgive me?"

"Forgive you?" asked Pete Reeve. "No, curse you, I'll never forgive you! You've sat with Dunkin around the fire. You've had chuck with him. Now you grab him for a reward."

"You're wrong, Pete," answered the giant. "I swear I won't take a cent of the reward, not a cent. That isn't my reason."

"You lie," cried Reeve. "I've trusted you like a brother, and here's my reward. I've loved you like a son, but now I give you my word that I'll never step off your trail, Bull, till I get you under my gun, and then one of us goes down for keeps."

"I'll never fight you," said Bull solemnly, and he yearned to see the face of the little man below the rock.

"You coward!" retorted Reeve. "Then I'll tell the whole range you're yaller to the core."

"It looks to me," said Bull mournfully, "like it's good bye. But I'll tell you this. Dunkin's no good. He never was any good. He's shot men from behind. He's robbed poor men. He's cheated with dice and cards. I've seen him when he cheated you, Pete, at your own camp fire. In spite of all that I would never have touched him if it hadn't been that one person in the world asked me. I had to do it. Will you give me a chance and try to understand

200

me? Old man, if you knew that . . . !"

A harsh oath cut him short. "Stop whining," called Reeve. "If you're half a man, give Dunkin back to me, or show yourself and fight me for him. Will you do that?" His voice quivered with rage and entreaty.

"I can't."

"Then heaven help one of us when we meet the next time!"

Bull hesitated. He loved this man who had been half father and half brother to him. "Pete," he said huskily, "will you listen to me say ten words?"

"If they're man talk, go ahead."

"Pete, you can't keep up the life you're leading. They's no hope for it. You can beat the law nine times. The tenth time it'll beat you, and it only needs to beat you once to end you. Get out of this country and. . . ."

"Say," shouted Pete Reeve, "are you sermonizing me?"

Bull Hunter turned the head of Diablo away and rode gloomily across the plateau, with Dunkin helpless on the saddle before him.

# IX

## "FOR THE WHIM OF A WOMAN"

In the town of White River they still tell how Bull Hunter brought in Dunkin. Fear, weariness, and his uncomfortable position on the horse had made Dunkin wilt, and the celebrated robber and killer was a limp rag of a man when Bull Hunter literally handed him over to the sheriff. The latter made preparations for Bull to secure the reward put on the head of Dunkin, but the giant refused absolutely to touch it. "A lady asked me to bring him in," he said, "so I did it."

Then he turned joylessly on the trail back to the Dunbar ranch. It was several days later when he reached it and, having had one bitter experience from blundering upon the house, he used some discretion on this occasion. After all, it was a surprisingly easy thing to do. He had only to wait in the shelter of the densest growth of trees until the men, to the very last one, had ridden out to their work of the day. A little patience showed him Mary Hood walking in the garden. He waited until she was screened from the house by a hedge, and then he went out to her. He came rather diffidently but, the moment the girl saw him, she ran to him.

"Did you do it?" she asked eagerly. "How? When?"

She literally danced about him with impatience for his answer. Bull Hunter gazed at her in dismay and wonder and delight. Again she was dressed in white, all white from the soft hat on her head to her shoes. The wind kept a stir of silk about her, and her excitement made her smile and laugh and frown, all in a moment. It was only the third time that he had seen her, but she had apparently decided to let all barriers fall at once. Here, in a stride, he found himself admitted to her intimate friendship. Looking back to the long labor of the hunt for Dunkin, the capture, and even the parting with Pete Reeve, these were small things.

"Yes," he was able to answer her at last. "I did it."

"But how? I want to know every bit of it."

Bull Hunter raised his face into the wind, as though hoping that it might bring him inspiration. "There isn't much to it," he said. "I just got on his trail, warned him I was coming and what I was going to try to do, and then I happened to catch him and bring him into the town of White River."

"That's all there is to it?" asked the girl, smiling faintly.

"That's all."

She broke out at him laughing. "But I know the whole story, Charlie. I know how you followed him and caught him in a noose, with that terrible Pete Reeve not far away, and I know how you rode into White River. And I know you refused the reward. It was a fine thing to do. It was a brave thing to do, Charlie, and the whole range is talking about it." She stopped, a little afraid that her enthusiasm had made her go too far, but one glance at his flushed, embarrassed face reassured her. "But you are not rich, and yet you refused a two-thousand dollar reward. Why did you do that? The money is yours."

"Of course I couldn't take it," answered Bull Hunter. "I'd already been paid for the job."

"Paid for it?"

"Yes."

He raised a hand to his throat and presently lifted above the edge of his shirt a thin chain of gold. She knew that was how he kept her locket. In spite of herself she flushed. There were so many qualities of modesty, gallantry, pride, and simplicity about this giant of a man that he continually took her by surprise.

"That's a pleasant thing to say to me," she answered softly. "Thank you."

"Besides," continued Bull, who had not quite finished with his thought, "if there is any reward coming, it would have to come from you."

She regarded him with something of a smile. Perhaps he was not quite so simple as she had suspected. "In what way?" she asked him.

"In a lot of ways," said Bull. "But first I'd like to know why you were so anxious to catch him."

"Because he had taken that locket, of course," she replied.

"No. I was bringing you the locket when you asked me to go for him. You gave me the locket for taking him."

She was stopped completely. "I don't like examinations," she told him with a frown. "To tell you the truth, I didn't really care a whit about it. But you seemed so eager to do something for me, and that thing happened to pop into my mind."

"You didn't have a real reason for wanting to have him caught?" asked Bull Hunter in amazement.

She explained: "You looked so big and so young and so strong that day that, just for a moment, I felt as if I were the lady and you were the knight out of some old story book. So I sent you to capture the villain, and the only villain I could think of, you see, was this Dunkin, the robber." She went on: "My father is almost willing to forgive you for the old quarrel, because you took Dunkin in such a clever way. As he says, Dunkin will never be able to hold up his head again. He'll be laughed out of the mountains by his own companions."

She stopped. The face of Bull Hunter was very grave.

"It sort of drifts in on me, little by little," he said slowly. "You didn't have no real reason for wanting Dunkin taken. It just popped into your mind?"

He walked up and down, and the girl, looking at the huge strides, the head bent in thought, and the heavily puckered forehead, lost a little of her elation. Presently he stopped before her again. He had been worshipping her beauty every moment of their talk, but now she saw a shadow in his eyes, and she was alarmed. It was not, she told herself at once, that she cared particularly for this big, dull-witted fellow, but — she found it impossible to define what she did feel. With the solemn eyes of the big man resting upon her, she had a positive reaction of guilt.

"Mary Hood," he said at length, "that was a long trail and a hard one. There were three men that might have died, instead of just one being captured unhurt, till the law hurts him. I didn't know why you wanted him taken. I didn't ask. Just that you wanted it was enough for me, and it still is. I'll forget what's happened. I'll forget that Dunkin is in jail and due to hang. . . ."

"But he's not in jail," broke in the girl. "Surely you heard what happened?"

"Eh?" asked Bull Hunter.

"Of course he's not in jail. He wasn't in White River a single night. You see, that terrible little man, Pete Reeve, rode down out of the mountains and, in the middle of the night, attacked the jail. He shot down two of the guards and left them badly wounded, then he set Dunkin free."

Bull Hunter closed his eyes, smiling faintly. He could see that picture, the little active gunfighter in his glory, storming the jail, the spit and bark of the guns, the crunching of bullets against the old brick walls of the jail. "Then they rode away together?" he asked.

"Dunkin rode away, but not Pete Reeve."

"What?"

He came close to her, grown terrible all at once. He stretched out his hands for the explanation, as though he were stretching them out to seize and crush her. She had never before been able to understand, in spite of his bulk, how this mild-voiced fellow could ever be formidable to fighting men. But a full realization of what he might be in action came suddenly to her and dazed her.

"Not Pete Reeve?" asked Bull Hunter, still following her as she shrank away.

"Does he mean as much to you as all that?"

"As much as that? As much as the world! He's saved my life and made me a man and taught me everything I know and been my friend. What's happened to him?"

"It happened in the jail . . . I don't know. It just came to me by hearsay, and there's nothing definite."

He turned gray with fear and suddenly caught her hands. "They killed Pete Reeve?" he asked. Then his voice thundered: "They killed Pete Reeve! I'll break a dozen of 'em to bits for it. They killed him! Pete Reeve is dead!"

"No, no! I give you my word. What I heard was that a bullet grazed his head and then knocked him unconscious. . . ."

"Dunkin stayed over the body like a brave man," said Bull in his agony. "Dunkin stayed there and fought them off. He stayed till Pete Reeve got his senses back, and then they fought their way through and got clear, tell me that was what happened?"

He still held her hands, and his face showed a dozen emotions. The girl shrank from him in her distress. There was as much difference between the placid Bull Hunter, whom she had known before, and this raging giant as the difference between a June sky and a thunderstorm.

"I wish I could say it. That was what you would have done, I know. You'd have stayed and fought them off for your friend. But Dunkin whom Pete Reeve had just saved, when he saw his friend drop, simply turned and ran for his life and rode away on Reeve's horse."

The chin of Bull Hunter dropped on his breast, and his hands fell limply away from hers.

"But is it so terrible? Won't he be able . . . ?"

"He'll hang," said Bull Hunter simply. "He's killed ten men, all in fair fight, and not a one of 'em but deserved the killing. But his record is long and black. This is the end of Pete Reeve." He lifted his head. "Unless I could do something!" he whispered. "Oh, if I could do something!"

She caught a dizzy glimpse into the future. She saw the giant, plunging on the guards at the jail in White River. "But they've changed everything. Since Dunkin got away, they have half a dozen men sleeping in the front room of the jail. You won't do some mad thing?"

"Mary Hood," he said, "Pete Reeve has been my partner."

There was no answer to this. All her arguments dried up in her throat and left her staring blankly at him. She felt, as she had never felt before, the mighty power of the friendship between man and man. It made the people she had grown up with seem paltry creatures. What would her father do for a friend in need? What would Hal Dunbar himself, for all his might of hand, do in the service of a man whose life was threatened by the law? But here was one who would risk his own life.

A panic took her, and yet she was thrilling with happiness at the thought of him. When her eyes cleared, she saw that he was holding out his hand and, when she extended hers to meet it, she felt the locket and gold chain drop into her palm, still warm from the body of the giant. She stared at him without understanding.

"I'll never see you again," said Bull Hunter. "Maybe I'll get bumped off when I try to bust the jail. Maybe not. But my trail will never come back here. Now that I'm going, I'll talk frank to you. I've loved you, Mary. I've worshipped you. I've kept you in front of me night and day. The thought of you kept me honest when I was living with thieves. And just a wish, that you wouldn't explain, made me go out and risk three men's lives and lose my friend. I didn't care. A touch of your hand was worth more to me than all of that. Now, just for a whim of yours, Pete Reeve is dead . . . worse than dead. Because, all the days he's in there at that jail, he's bound to think of what's coming to him. He was meant for a death under an open sky. He was meant for a fighting death that other men would never forget. Because of you he's trapped.

"I see you for the first time. There's no thought in you except for yourself. There's no generosity in your nature. You never think of giving but always of taking."

She tried to pull back from him. She wanted desperately to turn and flee to the house, but the steady, sad voice still held her. "You've taught me one thing that may be worth all the rest. They ain't a thing in the world after this that I can trust because of what it seems to be. Not a thing! I'll forget what trusting people means. And the worst of it is, I know that I'll keep on loving you, Mary Hood, to the end of my life."

Then he was gone. She saw him swing across the garden and disappear among the trees. Presently she heard the rush of a galloping horse through the underbrush. The locket slipped from her hands, struck the catch in its fall, and lay open at her feet. Mary Hood stamped on the lovely face of the miniature and turned and fled to the house.

# X

## "THE CHOICE"

There was cruel work for Diablo on that back trail to the town of White River, for Bull Hunter rode like a madman, hardly stopping for food and sleep. When they reached the little village, Bull went straight to the jail.

The moment he set foot in the street it was apparent that the town considered him a distinguished visitor. He saw women in gingham come to doors and stand with their arms akimbo, smiling and nodding at him. A boy ran fearlessly out and strove to shake hands with him as he swept by. A little crowd gathered in his wake, like dust behind a wind, and followed him to the jail.

When he went through the door, he was accorded a real reception. The half-dozen guards, of whom Mary Hood had spoken, proved to be only three. They sat in the front room of the jail, armed to the teeth with rifle, revolver, and even prominently displayed knives. Plainly the next visitor who came unannounced to the White River jail would be accorded a reception he would never forget.

The sheriff introduced Bull to the guards, and they shook hands with the carelessness of Westerners who wish to prove that they are not overly impressed on meeting a distinguished man. But Bull Hunter was too unhappy to notice. The sheriff immediately afterward drew him into his little office.

"I've news for you, Hunter," he said, "and great news at that. You surprised me a good deal when you wouldn't take that two thousand on the head of Dunkin. A good thing for you that you didn't, because Dunkin would have been gone before you got the money. But there's better game than that for you, Hunter, a lot better."

He settled back in his chair and smiled benevolently upon the giant. "Matter of fact, we want men like you around White River. If I had a fellow like you to call on as a deputy, now and then, when a hard job comes up, there'd be such a falling off in crime around these parts that it'd make your head swim. Yes, sir! Now, Hunter, I've been in touch with the authorities to find out if there's any need of paying the reward on the head of Pete Reeve. The man whose bullet stunned him won't get it, wouldn't take it if he could, because he happens to be the richest man in these parts. But we all figured it out that, if you hadn't taken Dunkin, Reeve would never have come in and practically put himself in our hands, so to speak. That reward needs a taker and, with a little work on the side, I think I could get it for you. In return for that. . . ."

"Sheriff," broke in Bull Hunter, "it's kind of you to think of all this, but I don't want the reward."

The sheriff gaped.

"You see," said Bull Hunter, "I've just come in to look things over, to see if Reeve was really here, that's all."

They were interrupted by the sound of a blast behind the building.

"Chopping out a foundation for a new jail," explained the sheriff. "Want to see it?"

Bull assented and, as they went out and around the building, the sheriff went on: "This old jail of ours is a pretty rickety affair. One of these days them brick walls'll tumble down. We'd been figuring on putting up a new one for some time, and that little jail-busting stunt of Reeve's woke us up. Boys been hard at the foundations ever since. We're going to have a cellar, as you see. Main trouble is that they hit rock right under the surface, and they're having to bite it out with powder. Hello, there's a whopper!"

They had come around to the rear of the jail by this time, and they saw two men struggling out with a ponderous jagged rock that had been torn loose by the last explosion. Other rocks in piles and heaps of dirt had been taken from a small rectangular excavation.

"The new walls are going to be stone," said the sheriff, "and then we'll have something that'll keep us safe and sound. Until that time," he went on, as they turned back, "we need good deputies handy. Wonder if you'd think about settling down here? Of course you don't mean what you said about refusing the reward. Why, man, add up all that's offered by some and sundry, and it comes to 'round about ten thousand."

"I'll think it over," said Bull. "Meantime I'd like to see Reeve, if I may."

The sheriff was perfectly cordial. He took Bull to the outer room and pointed to a door. "That leads to the jail room. Nobody but Reeve in it. He's got no weapons, of course. Think you could trust yourself in there alone with him?"

It was exactly what Bull wanted. He smiled, and the sheriff unlocked the door and waved Bull inside.

210

It was a low, square room, so dark that he could barely make out Pete Reeve, smoking unconcernedly at the far end of it. The sheriff closed the door, and they were alone. Pete Reeve, eyeing the visitor from head to foot, seemed to be quite unaware of his presence. Bull crossed the room to him and stood above the cot where the little man sat. He seemed smaller than ever. His hair was grayer. Now that the law had him in its grip, he seemed to have aged ten years. Put him out in the open, on a strong horse, and he would soon recover his vigor. Bull Hunter looked down on him with pity and a touch of horror.

"I don't expect you to talk to me, Pete," he said gently. "If you had a gun with you, I know the sort of talk you'd make. But you haven't, and I don't blame you much for not speaking. But the point is that Dunkin has shown himself the same sort of skunk that I told you he was. You thought he was worth fighting for . . . but he wasn't. He run off and left you cold in the lurch, Pete. That's his kind. I've come to tell you that I'm going to get you out or do something that'll put me in here with you."

There was one spark of light in the eyes of the little man. It went out almost at once. Then he said slowly: "How are you going to break in?"

"Through that wall," answered Bull instantly. He pointed to the back wall of the jail. "That door into the outside room opens back. Can you wedge it tonight, so's it can't be opened easy, in case the guards try to run in?"

Pete Reeve stood up suddenly and gripped the arm of the giant. "Why, boy," he answered, "I think you mean business. But what about the wall? You don't mean to come through a big brick wall?"

"I probably won't be able to," said Bull Hunter, "but I'm going to try. You do your part about the door."

"One thing else," said Pete Reeve. "Have you got a gun on

211

you beside the one in your holster?"

"I always have," said Bull. "You taught me that, Pete."

The little man rubbed his hands in an ecstasy. "Good boy! Bull, if I cussed you out the other day, it was because I was edgy about the way you nabbed Dunkin. It was an unpartnerly thing to do, eh?"

"It was," admitted Bull humbly.

"But it wasn't either," retorted Pete Reeve, who apparently disliked agreement of any kind. "Dunkin was a skunk. Too bad you didn't drop that rope around his neck in place of his shoulders. I got to keep on learning new things about men till I'm a hundred years old, I guess. But the gun, Bull. Give me that extra gun, and I'll do my own share about getting myself out."

Bull shook his head. "When we make the break tonight, we're going to get away without shooting a gun or else let ourselves drop without firing back. Is that straight to you, Pete?"

"It's crazy, that's what it is. No sense to it. Whoever heard of breaking jail without a gun play?"

"We'll make history then," replied Bull Hunter. "What I say goes tonight."

"Not in a thousand years."

"Are you going to stay and wait for the rope? Rather do that than die full of good, honest lead?"

"Stop, Bull," said Reeve. "The hangman's knot is tied under my ear every night in my dreams. You win, Bull. What you say goes for tonight."

Bull shook hands with him silently, and they parted.

# XI

## "THE TWO VERSIONS"

There were two versions of what happened that night in White River, that most historic of all nights in the town. The one is the version of Mrs. Caswell; and the other is the version of the sheriff. Mrs. Caswell lived in the little house opposite the rear of the jail. As she told the story, the night was so very warm that she could not sleep. Moreover, being an older woman of sixty-five, her sleep at all times was easily disturbed. She tossed in her bed for a long time and finally got up and put on a dress and went to sit on her little verandah and watch the stars. Because, as she said, stars are "tolerable quieting when you pick 'em out, one by one, and look hard."

This night, however, the stars were dimmed by the whitest of white moonshine. So brilliant was the moon, indeed, that it dazzled the eyes of Mrs. Caswell. She looked down to the earth instead. So it happened that she saw a giant out of a fairy tale walk slowly up to the rear of the jail. He was so huge, even at that distance, that she adjusted her glasses and stared again to make sure.

This huge man, having come to the rear of the jail, looked about him for a moment, as though searching for something on the ground. At length he seemed to have found what he wanted. He stooped and rose again, bearing a large object in his hands. With this he approached the rear wall of the jail. There she saw him brace his legs far apart and then swing the object, which was of great size, above his head.

Once, twice, and again he struck the wall of the jail, and the dull sound of the blows came to her distinctly. Following the last there was a rush and a roar and a ragged section of the wall collapsed, exposing the dark interior. Out of this darkness a small figure darted, small as a child beside the giant, and the two raced across the open.

At the same time a great hubbub broke out from the front of the jail, and presently other men plunged through the dark gap in the rear wall and ran after the two fugitives, firing shots. The latter, however, came to two horses near some cottonwoods, swung into the saddles, and were at once gone at a racing pace. After which, Mrs. Caswell, her ears full of the sound of shots and yells and her mind full of giants and elves, collapsed.

The sheriff's narrative was even simpler. He sat among the three guards of the night shift waiting for the morrow, when his distinguished and formidable prisoner should be taken from his hands and carried to a safer prison. It was well after midnight. Everyone was fagged, and they drank coffee steadily to keep on the alert.

Without warning they heard a blow at the rear of the jail and felt a shock that shook the floor beneath them. They remained motionless, stunned with surprise. Someone said that it must be a blast from the excavation at the rear. The words were not out of his mouth when the blow and shock were repeated. The sheriff then sprang up and tried the door, but it failed to give under his hand and seemed to be securely wedged on the inside. At the same time there was another blow, this time accompanied by a great crashing and rending sound of falling brick, and the voice of Pete Reeve calling: "Good boy! That does it!"

The sheriff shouted. Two of his guards lunged at the door and knocked it open. When they reached the hole in the rear wall, the fugitives were far away in the moonlight and could not be brought down. There was a hot chase but a useless one.

They returned and examined the scene of the break, using lanterns. Here they found what the sheriff was certain was the implement used in breaking down the wall. It was a gigantic stone, with the face of it battered from the pounding against the bricks. Two of the sheriff's men essayed to lift it and succeeded only with the greatest difficulty. Accordingly they agreed that it would be impossible for any one man to use such a massive object as a tool to be swung in the hands. But everyone agreed that if there were such a man in the world capable of swinging that mass of rock above his head, it must be Bull Hunter and no other.

These details answered Mrs. Caswell's description of the giant, and the sheriff had a warrant for the apprehension of Bull Hunter, sworn out in due legal form, and a reward for his arrest was immediately added. It may be noted that the rock which Bull Hunter used as a hammer is now on exhibition in the new White River jail.

Bull Hunter and Pete Reeve rode for the mountains slowly, for all danger of pursuit was past, and they wished to save their horses. The Ghost scouted ceaselessly in wide circles, before and behind. As they rode, Bull Hunter talked long and earnestly. He came to an end as they reached the top of a hill, looking east, where the young morning was growing rosy.

"Advice, Bull, what advice can I give you?" asked Pete Reeve. "I know what you've done for me tonight is too much. But I'll tell you this. In a pinch a man is usually a man, unless he's a skunk like Dunkin . . . but a woman is always the first thing that comes into his mind. And one thing more, Bull. You ain't heard the last of Mary Hood."

# ETIAM IN MEDIAS RES

**Max Brand**® is the best-known pen name of Frederick Faust, creator of Dr Kildare™, Destry, and many other fictional characters popular with readers and viewers worldwide. Faust wrote for a variety of audiences in many genres. His enormous output totalling approximately thirty million words or the equivalent of 530 ordinary books, covered nearly every field: crime, fantasy, historical romance, espionage, Westerns, science fiction, adventure, animal stories, love, war, and fashionable society, big business and big medicine. Eighty motion pictures have been based on his work along with many radio and television programs. For good measure he also published four volumes of poetry. Perhaps no other author has reached more people in more different ways.

Born in Seattle in 1892, orphaned early, Faust grew up in the rural San Joaquin Valley of California. At Berkeley he became a student rebel and one-man literary movement, contributing prodigiously to all campus publications. Denied a degree because of unconventional conduct, he embarked on a series of adventures culminating in New York City where, after a period of near starvation, he received simultaneous recognition as a serious poet and successful popular-prose writer. Later, he traveled widely, making his home in New York, then in Florence, and finally in Los Angeles.

Once the United States entered the Second World War, Faust abandoned his lucrative writing career and his work as a screenwriter to serve as a war correspondent with the infantry in Italy, despite his fifty-one years and a bad heart. He was killed during a night attack on a hilltop village held by the German army. New books based on magazine serials or unpublished manuscripts continue to appear. Alive and dead he has averaged a new one every four months for seventy-five years. In the U.S. alone nine publishers issue his work, plus many more in foreign countries. Yet, only recently have the full dimensions of this extraordinarily versatile and prolific writer come to be recognized and his stature as a protean literary figure in the 20th century acknowledged. His popularity continues to grow throughout the world.